THE

"Think!"

"Think, damn you, think! Talk to me of Earth. Earth, man! Earth!"

Gourvich stared blankly into his cup, Dumarest falling silent as, abruptly, the old man lifted his head.

In a thin, cracked voice, his mouth twisted into a vacuous grin he chanted, "Thirty-two, forty, sixty-seven—that's the way to get to heaven. Seventy-nine, sixty, forty-three—are you following me? Forty-six, seventy, ninety-five—up good people, live and thrive!"

Madness?

The babblings of a deranged mind?

Or the coordinates of Earth?

Also in Arrow by E. C. Tubb

E. C. Tubb

THE COMING EVENT

ARROW BOOKS

To Maureen and Claire Harbottle

Arrow Books Limited
62-65 Chandos Place, London WC2N 4NW

An imprint of Century Hutchinson Ltd

London Melbourne Sydney Auckland
Johannesburg and agencies throughout
the world

First published in Great Britain by Arrow 1986

Printed and bound in Great Britain by
Anchor Brendon Limited, Tiptree, Essex

ISBN 0 09 944620 0

CHAPTER ONE

Buried deep beneath the scarred surface of a lonely world the cavern held the awesome grandeur of a legendary tomb—a tremendous mausoleum buttressed by massive columns which formed an adamantine protection for the soaring tiers of featureless ovoids within their embrace, though it was even now being despoiled by men and machines.

To Master Elge, Cyber Prime, the fabrication was the reverse of a tomb, the ovoids far from being coffins, but the desecration was real, and he watched as units were freed from their housings and swung down into the arms of waiting cradles to be wheeled silently away.

And each ovoid held a living, thinking brain.

This was the reward for which cybers dedicated their lives. They worked until they grew physically inefficient then were stripped of hampering flesh, their brains removed from their skulls and placed in containers, sealed from harm while fed with nutrients, at last hooked into series with others of their own kind to form a part of the tremendous complex which was the heart and power of the Cyclan.

But now Central Intelligence was threatened and with it the security of the whole.

"Twelve dozen units," said Jarvet from where he stood at Elge's side. "The entire section. As you instructed, Master."

And how many before them? Elge knew the exact number but even one would have been too many. "Results?"

"As yet totally negative."

"Numbers tested?"

"Eighteen selected at random." That was more than enough for a representative sample. The aide added, "I ordered a halt at twenty for your decision."

The aide could anticipate what the decision would be, Elge knew, but as his was the final responsibility his must be the deciding voice.

He turned, tall, thin, the scarlet robe shielding the taut lines of his body, maintained at optimum efficiency and carrying no surplus fat. To Elge as to all cybers food was to be used as fuel, eaten from necessity not pleasure. Training and an operation performed at puberty on the cortex had rid them of the capacity for emotion.

Jarvet fell into step behind him as Elge moved to a passage where a moving way carried them to a laboratory in which technicians worked over the freed ovoids. Many lay open to reveal their contents and Elge looked dispassionately at the convoluted brains rested beneath transparent covers amid their attendant mechanisms. Components designed never to fail. And they had not failed—the fault lay within the brains themselves.

But the fault was yet to be determined.

"Nothing, Master." Icelus gave his report. "No trace of any foreign bacteria or virus. No radiation-scarring or isotopic accumulation. No discernible tissue decay. No aggravated pressure zones. The Homochon elements are enlarged but only within anticipated parameters. No change in the cortex. Nothing can be discerned in the physical condition which could account for the aberration." He added, "The conclusions are as before."

At that time units had been sterilized with flame and reduced to their component atoms for fear of contamination, and examinations had been conducted in isolated areas by technicians who still remained isolated on distant worlds. Entire banks of machinery had been volatilized—Elge knew the details.

"Is there any traceable pattern?"

"No. The brains are old and that is the only thing we can be sure of."

"Any correlations?"

"None." Icelus was definite. "The thing seems to strike at random. These units are younger than the last yet older than the ones before. There is no similarity as to location or apparent vulnerability. These are from Bank 8 Tier 5. Those before came from Bank 3 Tier 9."

Different caverns and different positions—diversifying the units was an elementary precaution against total loss by unforeseen damage. Yet even that had provided no defense. The aberration must, somehow, be inherent. But what?

"Your orders, Master?" Icelus was waiting. "Shall I continue with the examinations?"

How often must he go over the same ground? There was a point beyond which any further effort would be worse than useless—efficiency demanded the full utilization of each and every facility and the technicians had other work.

Elge said, "Terminate."

"All, Master?"

"All." Every brain to be thrown into a furnace to be consumed by fire, the components dissolved into basic elements, the residue to be blasted deep into space. To Jarvet he said, "Order an assembly. I will meet the Council in an hour."

They sat at a long table, the warm hue of their robes the only touch of color in the bleakness of the chamber. Dekel was the first to speak, as Elge had predicted, but the mental achievement gave him little pleasure. The man was old, patterns established; the merest tyro could have done as well.

"This matter concerns Central Intelligence?"

"Yes."

"You have fresh information?" Boule was swift in his attack. "There is nothing to be gained by discussing what we already have covered."

Like Dekel and the rest, he was old, but that was to be expected—men did not achieve power without the passage of time. But age was relative and small signs betrayed when the fine edge had been crossed; the delicate balance between optimum efficiency and the insidious decline toward senility. Signs watched for by all as they all watched Elge. He with the highest office must demonstrate his ability to hold it.

From where he sat Therne said, "From my study of recent information I arrive at the conclusion that nothing new can be learned of the degeneration of the units by further examinations."

"Agreed. That is why I ordered a termination of all such activity." Elge continued, "There is no need to detail the negative findings. They are as before. Nor is there need to discuss extrapolations of probable consequences should the aberrations continue. The prediction of internal collapse based on an exponential curve leads to near-certain disaster."

This seemed so obvious as to need no comment.

Alder said, "Why have we been summoned?"

"To review the situation. Later I shall want from each of you detailed plans of optimum survival based on all possible contingencies. Now I wish to cover the base problem. From a summation of all findings relevant to the affected units it is logical to accept the premise that there is no mechanical or biological cause for the derangements. The brains involved failed because of some inherent fault other than external cause. Agreed?"

Boule demurred. "That need not necessarily be the case. Because we cannot find a cause does not mean that one does not exist."

"True, but all precautions have been taken as regards shielding and monitoring." Elge was curt. "I submit the fault could lie in the region of the psyche. To illustrate the point I have arranged for a demonstration." A communicator stood on the table before him. Activating the instrument he said, "Now."

Abruptly the room turned black.

It was the complete elimination of all light and for a moment they felt as if blinded and buried deep in a tomb, shielded for eons from the sun. Then, slowly, light came and with it an image.

It floated above the table; a three-dimensional hologram depicting a male, nude, set with wires which sprouted from his skull like the tendrils of some strange and oddly designed creature. The eyes were closed, sunken beneath prominent brows, the ears padded. Mouth and nose were covered by a mask and the medium in which he floated was not air or space.

"Water warmed and maintained at his individual body heat." The accompanying voice whispered through the chamber. "All senses have been blocked or negated so as to deny the intelligence any external stimuli. The electrodes on the skull relay the encephalic readings of the cortex."

Another picture joined the first; a depiction of wavering lines traced by delicate points. The wave pattern of the subject's brain, which all could read.

"Total disorientation was achieved in a remarkably short space of time," continued the voice. "Hallucinations followed leading to a complete catatonic withdrawal. Note the zeta and lambda lines." A pause, then, "Three hours later." A flick and the figure could be seen with knees drawn up to its chin, arms wrapped around the knees. "The classic fetal position. Twelve hours later when removed from the tank."

They looked at an idiot.

"Enough." Elge had no wish to stare at the drooling, vacuous-eyed, blank-faced vegetable. The point, surely, had been made. "The subject was of low intelligence," he explained. "Run as a comparison with others of a higher level of capability. The greater the intelligence the longer was individual awareness maintained."

Dekal said, "Your conclusion?"

"The derangement affecting the units has some relation to sensory deprivation."

After a moment Boule said, "We are talking of minds accustomed to a degree of sensory deprivation for the major part of their lives. And need I remind you that when sealed in their units they are provided with external stimuli in the form of communication with others of their kind together with cybers in rapport? I find the conclusion lacking in conviction."

Therne said, "If the matter is one of the need for external stimuli I agree there remains a doubt as to the validity of the conclusion. As sanity is being maintained the cause must lie elsewhere."

"Sanity is not being maintained," reminded Elge. "Not in all units at all times. If so there would be no problem. You have studied the recordings made of communication with affected units—what did you find?"

"Delusion," admitted Therne. "Ravings. Systems of logic built on false premises."

"Withdrawal. Intelligences disoriented and drifting in a void of speculation. A denial of accepted fact." Elge looked from one to the other. "I stand by my conclusion."

"That the aberrations are induced by sensory deprivation?"

"That a relationship could exist." Elge was precise. "If so it may be necessary to reaffirm established frameworks of reference. With this in mind I have taken steps to investigate the value of certain methods." Again he activated the communicator. "Continue."

This time the room didn't turn black but color and movement shone where there had been emptiness. The chamber was equipped, like an operating theater, with muted greens and sterile whites, with metal and plastic and the sheen of crystal. To one side lay an opened ovoid, the brain clearly visible. In the foreground stood a squat machine in the shape of a man. A grotesque parody with a domed head, rounded torso and oddly fashioned limbs. Around it, both robot and brain technicians worked in smooth coordination.

"Attempts to provide units with separate, operational vehicles have been made several times," explained the accompanying voice. "All have led to failure. A direct brain transplant to a human body is impossible because of the enlargement of the engrafted Homochon elements which takes place after the unit has been sealed into its container. The use of substitute physical hosts was tried and abandoned because of the low-return anticipated against the high-effort such attempts entailed. We are now attempting to couple the brain to a mechanical analogue of the human shape. Once the attachments have been made and activated the analogue will become an extension of the unit's intelligence. As yet we have had little success in this line of experimentation."

In the glowing depiction figures moved in accelerated tempo, wires and pipes and terminals meshing to form a complex web. A moment later the scene slowed to show the robot now standing alone. As they watched, it stirred, one arm lifting, to lower, to lift again. Then it paused like a child who has made a discovery and now broods over what it has found.

"The first reaction. Two hours later we had this."

The arm again, moving like a hammer, up and down, up and down. The dome of the head moved a little, the body tilting to allow the scanners set in the parody of eyes to stare upward at a brightly polished surface.

"Thirty-two minutes later."

A man hurtled through the air as a steel arm smashed into his chest and filled his lungs with splintered bone. Spewing blood he fell, tripping another, joined by a third with an oddly twisted neck. A fourth, head pulped, dropped like a stone as the robot moved. It swayed, turned, lurched forward, the massive arm lifting to slam down with crushing force, pulping the exposed brain, sending it to spatter in all directions.

In his office Elge touched a control and watched as a galaxy was born. The air filled with the cold glitter of countless points of radiance interspersed with sheets and curtains of luminescence, the ebon smudges of interstellar dust. A masterpiece of electronic wizardry; each mote of light held in a mesh of electromagnetic forces, the whole forming a compressed depiction of the galactic lens.

With such diminution details had to be lost; the billions of individual worlds, comets, asteroids, satellites, rogue planets, meteors, the drifting hail of broken suns. But the stars were present and, as he watched, scarlet flecks appeared in scattered profusion.

The power of the Cyclan.

A power vast and yet almost invisible. Each fleck represented a world which had lost self-determination in its reliance on the services provided by the Cyclan, though the planets were unaware of the trap into which they had fallen. It did not take an army to move a mountain when a touch could shift the stone which led to an avalanche. One touch could exert pressure where it would achieve the greatest gain, use persuasion and play on lust and greed, envy and hatred, anger and fear—all the weapons forged by emotion-cursed humanity against itself. The Cyclan stood aloof as it manipulated the destiny of captive worlds.

His power was hidden, unsuspected by most, but nonetheless real.

"Master." Jarvet had entered the office to stand beside the Cyber Prime, the blazing depiction illuminating his face, dotting it with rainbow patches. "The reports from Siguri and Guptua?"

These details could not be ignored. On Siguri a drunken young fool had threatened a cyber and had slapped him in the face, the act compounded in its folly by having been done in public. The physical injury was slight, but the man had committed an unpardonable crime.

Elge said, "From a check of his background it is obvious the culprit fears ridicule more than death. Order the failure of the crops on Heght. They provide the basis of his Family's income. At the same time seduce him into making heavy investments in the Chan-Pen Enterprise. It will fail and his House be ruined. He, himself, will be ostracized and villified."

This was using a hammer to crack a nut and yet no insult to any cyber could be allowed to pass unpunished. The fool would pay with ridicule and dishonor and final death by his own or another's hand. His Family would be disgraced and their power lost—payment for having given birth to the one who had struck the blow. All would know the details and, knowing, would fear the Cyclan. And with that fear would come enhanced respect.

"And Guptua?"

A world torn by internecine war as two brothers fought for a decaying throne. Elge gave orders which would ruin them both and place the future prosperity of the planet firmly in the grasp of the Cyclan. Details would be attended to by local cybers; he plotted the main strategies, but some things demanded his personal attention.

The mania of the brains.

His own fate should he fail to provide the solution.

Nequal had failed and now Nequal was dead and he occupied the vacated position. That position was determined by the vote of the Council and they would be watching for the slightest trace of inefficiency. Who would take his place should he fail? Icelus? No, the man was too circumscribed by his devotion to science. Jarvet? He was a good aide but lacked the subtle attribute which made a leader. Avro? A possibility, as was Marle.

Such speculation had no place and Elge recognized the danger. The love of power was reason enough for any cyber to be denied it and for the Cyber Prime most of all. For him, as for all, the Cyclan must be paramount.

Why had the robot destroyed the brain?

Suicide, Dekal had said, and he could be right, but that in itself was a demonstration of madness. What intelligent mind would seek self-destruction? This was another facet of the problem which had to be tested with further experiments but those were already underway.

The depicted galaxy seemed to expand as he manipulated a control; points of light streamed to all sides to paint transient paths of brilliance over robes and the bleak furnishings of the office. As movement halted greater detail became visible; a sun, planets, a world marked with a glowing arrow.

"Ascelius." Jarvet didn't look at the Cyber Prime. "Where Okos went insane."

A reminder Elge didn't need; he was fully aware of the problem. Aware too of the hammer-blow the incident had struck at the tower of confidence based on the efficiency of Central Intelligence.

It was impossible to tell which units of the gigantic complex were contacted by a cyber in rapport. Relaxing, he activated the implanted Homochon elements with the aid of the Samatchaze formulae and, once a certain stage had been reached, became as one with the massed brains. This union was beyond normal understanding; a merging, a belonging, a communion of minds. Knowledge was exchanged by a form of osmosis; a mental communication conducted at near-instantaneous velocity. This all cybers relished because of the mental intoxication experienced during the aftermath.

Yet Okos had gone insane.

Had he been flawed to begin with? A possibility but one so remote as to be negligible; any such weakness would have been discovered during his training as an acolyte. The impact of external stimuli? Again a remote possibility; a cyber was proof against the mental conflicts which destroyed ordinary men. His insanity could only have originated during rapport—a reflection of the aberration of deranged brains.

A madness which had allowed Dumarest to escape.

That failure merited a harsh penalty but death had put the cyber beyond that and beyond questioning, which could have provided valuable information. A loss but to dwell on it would be a futile waste of time.

And Dumarest had survived.

The depiction changed to show a new sector of the galaxy; a region of close-set suns and a host of worlds. The Zaragoza Cluster into which Dumarest had fled, there to move in a random pattern from world to world. A needle in a haystack but from which he had been lured.

And would soon be captured, the secret stolen from the Cyclan recovered, the man himself rendered into dust. Elge felt the warm glow of mental achievement as he predicted the immediate future. Once the affinity twin was in his hands the problem of the deranged brains would be solved if his suspicions were correct. Given host bodies the question of sensory deprivation would cease to exist. Would the brain have destroyed itself had it inhabited the body of a man?

A part of the whole; with the affinity twin every ruler and person of influence would become a puppet of a dominant cyber. World after world would fall beneath the domination of the Cyclan and the Great Plan would mature within decades instead of millennia.

Dumarest held the key to that vista.

Again the depiction changed to show a mote of light against a background of starred emptiness. Not a world but a man-made structure insignificant against the bulk of planets.

"Zabul." Jarvet echoed his confidence. "The home of the Terridae. A place from which Dumarest cannot escape. Cyber Lim reported him as good as captured."

"Not taken?"

"A preliminary report. The prediction was that he would be on the *Saito* within the hour."

Yet Lim had not reported the actual capture. Was he waiting until the vessel had left the vicinity? Had there been an unforeseen complication?

"Contact the *Saito*. Check with Central Intelligence to see that there has been no further rapport with Lim. Have all data appertaining to Zabul and the Terridae on my desk as soon as possible."

"Master?" Jarvet was puzzled. "You suspect something could have gone wrong?"

Elge remained silent. He was thinking of Okos.

CHAPTER TWO

In the dream a woman was laughing, a girl with a helmet of golden hair which hugged a face with strong bones, jaw and cheeks and eyebrows all denoting a stubborn strength. The eyes were blue and the mouth thinner than it should have been but the hands she held up before her were those of an artist.

"Look at this, Earl!" The hands moved to pick up a painting and he stared at the depiction of a young boy with thick curly hair and a mouth like a pouting rosebud. A mute he had once known.

"And this!" A portrait of a man sitting at a window staring at distant hills. He was dressed all in grey with the hilt of a knife riding above his right boot and the mark of a killer stamped in the set of mouth and eyes.

"And this!" An old crone seated on a box adorned with esoteric symbols.

"And these! These, damn you! These!"

She thrust out hands that were crushed and broken, blood oozing from ripped nails, more from ruptured ligaments, wrists puckered with gaping mouths of agony.

"Earl! Earl!"

The voice faded, ending in a blaze of white then returning again in a tone not belonging to the woman standing at his side.

"Earl! What is wrong? You were screaming, crying out." Pausing, Althea Hesford added, "You sounded almost like a woman."

15

The dream woman had been Carina Davaranch whom he had taken and used with the magic of the affinity twin. To send her to torture and final death. Did a ghost remember? Could the dead mourn the broken hands which made it impossible to paint?

"Earl?"

"It's nothing." Dumarest reared to sit upright in the bed. "A dream. A nightmare. It isn't important."

"Are you sure?"

He nodded, closing his eyes, seeing again the face framed in the helmet of golden hair. He had dominated her mind and she had died and he had returned to his own body—had a part of her returned with him?

"The Council is meeting," said Althea. "I came to warn you. I thought you'd need time to prepare. And I thought you'd like this."

She had brought a tray containing a pot of tisane together with small cakes, some spiced, others with the flavor and consistency of ground nuts. Dumarest poured a cup of tisane and sat nursing it, inhaling the fragrant steam as he waited for it to cool.

Sitting down beside him, Althea said, "It isn't going to be easy, Earl. The young want you to lead them but the Elders are against it. If we could force a vote I think you'd win, but a full referendum will take time to arrange and delay could cost you the advantage."

Politics—the curse of civilization. Dumarest tasted the tisane and found it cool enough to swallow. It filled his mouth and stomach with a scented warmness and, rising, he headed into the bathroom to shower. Dried, he returned to the bedroom and dressed. Althea watched him with wide-spaced, luminous green eyes, the copper mane of her hair accentuating the delicate pallor of her face. She wore gold, a high-necked gown which fell to below her knees and was caught at the waist with a belt of heavy links. Against the fabric the contours of breasts and hips were sharply delineated. The skirt, slit at one side, revealed the long curves of her thigh at every second step.

A lovely woman but she had never known the tribulations of a normal world.

"Earl!" She barred his passage as he headed toward the door. "Good luck, darling."

Her kiss held a smoldering passion, which he had shared in the past and would share again, but now Dumarest had more urgent matters to attend to. Outside he turned left and moved down a spacious corridor to a flight of stairs. At its foot a group of young people saluted him. Some he recognized. One, Medwin, he knew well.

"We're with you, Earl," Medwin said. "If you want help just ask for it. If it needs force to kick the Council into action we can provide it."

"Guide us to the Event, Earl!" called another. "Lead us to Earth!"

Earth was the paradise they dreamed of, the world of eternal peace and happiness where all things would be given for the asking, the place of floating cities and soaring towers of crystal and benign Shining Ones, of pools into which the old and ugly could bathe to become young and beautiful. A planet of fantasy, fabricated by dreams, composed of eternal longings; it had never existed but they would never believe that. They, all of the Terridae, longed for the Event—the time when they would find Earth, the imagined heaven.

And they were convinced Dumarest could take them to it.

A conviction he'd helped to foster, for here, in the Archives and in the minds of those now dreaming in their caskets, must surely lie the clues he needed to find the planet of his birth.

There was no day in Zabul, no night; the collection of empty hulls and constructed spaces all united into an airtight whole circled no sun. Illumination came from artificial sources; a blue-white glow rich in ultraviolet coupled with warm reds and oranges which gave the illusion of sunrises and sunsets. Only in private chambers was it ever wholly dark. And, everywhere, on walls and ceilings and inset into floors, was the depiction of life in all its forms.

Those in the council chamber were of fish; the denizens of watery deeps together with rocks and weed and convoluted shells. The walls themselves, carefully shaped and painted, resembled an undersea dome. Those sitting at the table seemed as cold as the water itself; old, sere, bitter with eyes like fragments of yellowed ice. These were the Elders of the Terridae, the Council of Zabul, and studying them, Dumarest was aware of a change. The last time he had stood before them they had been his judges—now they had been judged, weighed in the balance and found wanting.

Urich Volodya had held the scales.

He stepped forward as Dumarest glanced toward him, tall, conscious of his power but knowing better than to display it. Volodya had recognized his opportunity and seized it, using Dumarest and his claim to gain the support of the young. He now made his position clear.

"Earl Dumarest, given the opportunity will you guide the Terridae to Earth?"

"The opportunity and the means—yes."

"Your needs?"

"Access to all records. The power to question all of the Terridae. The right to requisition all necessary labor and material."

Volodya said dryly, "Is that all? It seems you ask to become a dictator."

"If you want a man to do a task it is pointless to deny him the means to do it. I suggest you make that clear to the Council."

"There is no longer a Council of Zabul. Those forming it have agreed to retire to their caskets. Instead there will be a committee of seven with myself at the head. These changes have been forced on us by various pressures," he explained. "To resist them would have been to invite disaster. In their wisdom the retiring Council recognized that."

Aided by the persuasion of the guards under Volodya's command. As the only organized force in Zabul their arguments would have been irresistible.

Dumarest said, "A wise move. I commend it. The committee, naturally, will be formed to represent the whole. Two of the young, two of the old and two from the middle-age group. The sexes equally divided. Is Althea Hesford one of the committee?"

"Yes. Why do you ask?"

"She's deserved the appointment." Dumarest met Volodya's eyes. "Do you agree to my conditions?"

"As long as you do not endanger Zabul or the Terridae you will have a free hand. Althea Hesford will provide liaison." Volodya added, "I suggest you avoid all unnecessary delay."

Do it quickly—it would have to be that.

Like a city, Zabul had grown. The original concept bore additions which had overlaid the smooth ovoid dotted with spires into the bizarre assembly it now was: a compilation which held elements of lunacy.

Why did this passage turn to twist in on itself like a corkscrew? What had dictated the placement of this chamber? From where did this installation draw its power? How did this compartment harmonize with its twin?

Such details filled endless charts, maps, intricate schematics over which Dumarest pored for hours on end.

Althea grew impatient.

"Why do it, Earl?" she demanded. "What is the point? All you need do is issue orders and others will see they are carried out. There's no need for you to know every detail of Zabul."

She stood against one wall of the chamber he had made his office, the copper sheen of her hair bright against a scene of muted storm. The emerald of her gown matched the hue of her eyes.

Dumarest said, "How long have you waited for the Event?"

"All my life. Why?"

"And others?"

"As long—longer." She frowned, understanding his meaning. "You're telling me not to be impatient, is that it?"

"Yes."

"All right, I'll be patient, but I still can't see the need for all this." Her gesture embraced the papers lying thick on the long table at which he sat. "What are you looking for?"

The answers to questions she hadn't even imagined and Dumarest was cautious in his explanations. To tell her he was familiarizing himself with a potential battleground would be to strain her new-formed loyalty, and even if she said nothing Volodya was too shrewd not to scent a mystery. Once alerted he would move to safeguard his position and, from then, it would be a logical step to remove the source of potential danger.

That confrontation Dumarest hoped to avoid but he wanted to be ready to meet it if it came.

Now he said, "I was hoping to find an easy way to reach Earth. In the old days Zabul could be moved as an entire unit." He reached for a schematic and tapped various points with a finger. "See? These are the generators and this was the original navigation room and here would have been the computer installation. The captain would have operated from here. You see?"

"I think so." She bit her lip as she tried to visualize familiar installations with their prime intention. "Could it still be done?"

"I don't think so. Who should I ask to be certain?"

His name was Ivan Quiley; he was no longer young but was too interested in machines to idle away his life in casket-given dreams. He shook his head as Dumarest asked the question.

"No, Earl, it can't be done."

"Too many extensions?"

"You've hit it. The scope of the Erhaft field will no longer embrace all of Zabul. Even if we adjusted the conduits to feed maximum power into the generators the damage would be too great."

"And if the generators should be resited?"

"In theory almost anything will work," said Quiley dryly. "Move the generators, establish coordinated control systems and boost the power. Yes, it could be done, but it would need time and labor and material. Say the full efforts of all technicians for a couple of years at the very least."

Time he didn't have. Dumarest said, "Would it be possible to reach a compromise? I'm thinking of a field-jump effect."

Althea said, "What's that? I don't understand."

"A temporary application of the Erhaft field." Quiley didn't look at her. "Use it and you can move a short distance in space before the synchronization fails. It's possible, yes. As I said, most things are possible."

"I'm talking of days," said Dumarest. "A few weeks at the most. Supposing Zabul ran into danger—what then?"

"We're in a selected drift node," explained Quiley. "There's no gravitation drag to draw us to any world or sun. We could stay in this position until the universe ran down. Once it was established and proved there was no need for us to move." He added, almost as an afterthought, "Of course we have defenses."

Installations which could send missiles to vaporize any threatening scrap of debris. Men trained to working in void conditions. Teams which could disperse to defend Zabul from unwanted visitors.

That was the best Dumarest could hope for. Rising, he said, "Check on all equipment and keep it on operational alert. Double the observers and arrange for alternative sources of power to all essential installations."

Quiley grunted as he made notes. Without looking up from his memo pad he said, "I'll recheck the possibility of locating the generators in more favorable positions. Maybe, if we cut down some of the extensions and ran wave-grids down passages 27 through to 92, the field could be extended for a short-term use at least. I'll see to it."

As he left Althea said, "He's on your side, Earl. Most of the technicians are."

"Most?"

"Some want to hang on to the old ways. They think you threaten their importance. Once we reach Earth what will they have to do?"

Dumarest left the question unanswered; the anxieties of potentially redundant technicians were the least of his worries.

Always Zabul held sound; the muted susurration of trapped vibrations echoing and harmonizing to form a medley which could be translated by the imagination into subtle music, mathematical sequences or abstract resonances. A noise not even noticed by those accustomed to it, but now it held something new. A harsh, martial sound which grew as Dumarest neared the gymnasium, to flower into cries, the clash of metal and stamp of feet, the harsh yells of command from the instructors he had trained.

"In! Get in there! Attack! Delay could cost you victory!"

On the cleared floor two dozen men faced each other in a dozen pairs. Each was naked aside from shorts, all armed with a short bar of metal; dummy knives held sword-fashion, thumb to the blade and point held upward. Many carried ugly weals and dark bruises. One had a broken nose; dried blood masking mouth and chin. Several bore trails of blood from lacerated scalps.

"Horrible!" At his side Althea voiced her disgust. "Earl, is this necessary? To turn men into beasts?"

"You would rather they died?"

"Who is to hurt them? Earth is a haven of peace. They have no need to train as butchers."

Dumarest said patiently, "I've explained all that. Before we can enjoy your haven of peace we have to get there. Others might object." He lifted his voice as the men prepared to reengage. "Erik! Hold the action!"

Medwin came toward him, smiling, face and torso beaded with sweat. A long scrape ran over his ribs and a bruise rested over his navel.

"Earl! Glad you could drop in. What do you think of our progress?"

The truth would have been cruel and they were not to blame for their ignorance. Even Volodya's guards knew little of martial arts, relying on acceptance of their authority more than their skill with club and gas-gun.

Reaching out Dumarest touched the long scrape, the mottled bruise.

"If you'd fought for real you'd be dead by now. And so would most of those others down there. Here, let me show you."

Stripped, Dumarest joined the others and, watching, Althea noted the differences. Not just his superior height or the hard musculature of his body but his stance, the feral determination which dictated every move. Beneath the lights the tracery of cicatrices on his torso made a lacelike pattern, scars earned during the early days of his youth when he had learned the skill he was now trying to pass on.

"You!" He pointed to a man with broad shoulders and a narrow waist, who was as yet unmarked. "Ready? Attack!"

Kirek was confident, proud of his physical development, eager to score. He blinked as his thrust met no resistance, grunted as metal slammed against his side, backed as the bar darted toward him to halt with the point touching his throat.

"Let's do it again," said Dumarest.

This time he stood, waiting arms outstretched at his sides. A tempting target and, smarting with his recent defeat, Kirek rushed in.

To stumble as Dumarest moved deftly aside, to fall as, pushed, he tripped over an outthrust foot.

"You've got a choice," said Dumarest as the man climbed to his feet. "You can make excuses or you can admit you need to learn. If you want to make excuses then you've no place here."

"You were fast," muttered Kirek. "So damned fast I didn't see you move."

"Well?"

"I—" Kirek swallowed, then threw back his shoulders. "I guess I need to learn."

"Good. The first thing to bear in mind is that this isn't a game. When you face a man, armed or not, recognize the fact that he wants to kill you. It's your life or his. If you want to stay alive you have to hit first, hit hard and make the blow tell. To hesitate is to give your opponent an advantage. To aim to hurt and not to kill, the same. To do either is to invite death." To Kirek he said, "What did you do wrong?"

"I rushed in. You looked too easy. I guess I underestimated you."

"And maybe you wanted to show off a little, right?" Dumarest smiled, removing the sting from the rebuke. "It's a natural reaction. Now let's do it again and this time remember what I said."

This time he made no concessions, crouching in a fighter's stance, poised on the balls of his feet, the bar of metal held before him, point upward, the metal slanted to one side. Had it been a real knife the hold would have given the opportunity to slash in a variety of directions, to thrust, to turn so as to catch and reflect the light. His face matched the stance, falling unconsciously into the bleak mask of a man determined to kill, fighting for his life.

Kirek tried to copy him, a tyro against a veteran, but he had the elements and was willing to learn.

Dumarest opened the encounter, doing as he would never have done in a ring, moving to touch his dummy knife against the other's and by so doing presenting him with an opportunity.

One he took, moving in to knock Dumarest's bar aside with his own weapon before lunging forward in a vicious thrust.

Metal rang as Dumarest parried, striking back in turn, the slash deliberately slow and falling short by an inch. Kirek parried the proffered weapon, cut at Dumarest's stomach, missed and, too late, tried a backhanded slash. He grunted as

Dumarest weaved, dodging the attack to slap his own bar of metal against Kirek's side.

"I win," said Dumarest. "Resent it?"

"No, of course not, but—"

"You were good," said Dumarest. "And you can be better. All it needs is practice. But you're all trying to rush things. Erik!"

"Earl?"

"Keep them at basic drill for a while. You've matched them too soon. Wait until they have mastered the basic movements and can do them without conscious thought. Then have them go through routine attacks and parries. If they learn bad habits now they'll be hard to get rid of later." He added, seeing the shadow in the young man's eyes, "But you've done well. Far better than I'd hoped for. You're just a little too impatient."

"Can you blame us for that?"

"No, but it takes time to train a man. Once you've taught these they can teach others. That goes for all of you." He glanced at the men, the other instructors. "Just don't try to run before you can walk."

The noise rose again as, dressed, Dumarest walked with Althea from the gymnasium. In a small enclosure filled with plants and heavy with the scent of flowers she halted and sat on a bench.

As he joined her she said, "You were kind in there, Earl. You could have made Alva look a fool."

"Alva?"

"The man you fought. Alva Kirek. He is Volodya's nephew. You didn't know that?"

Dumarest shook his head; the relationships of the Terridae were a mystery to him, but he saw no point in solving it. Marriage, family life, personal loyalties—all must be strange when conducted among those who spent the major part of their lives in ornamented caskets waiting for the culmination of a dream.

"You were kind," said Althea again. "Against you he was slow and clumsy and you could have made him a laughing-stock. The lesson might have done him good."

Dumarest said, "It never pays to make an enemy. I want that man on my side not against me." This was a slip and he cursed the fatigue which had led him to make it. "We need dedicated men," he said. "Those who will be willing to endure hardship."

"Men willing to kill?"

"Men willing to fight," he corrected. "To reach out for what they want. To destroy those who try to stop them."

"Violence."

"Protection." He turned to face her, looking at the face blurred in the dim illumination, the wide, luminous pools of her eyes. "Without it what do you have? The trust that others will not harm you? The hope you will be ignored and left to go your own way? Your ancestors knew better. They knew that all life is a continual act of violence. Why else did they build Zabul?"

"As a haven."

"True, but an armed one. In the beginning it was a fortress designed to safeguard the Terridae in their caskets. How else to ensure protection from fire and flood and war? From quakes and natural hazards? Where better to wait as the years drifted by and the Event came nearer? But they weren't prepared just to wait. The original plans make it clear what they intended."

"But we bred," she said. "Grew in numbers—can we be blamed for that?"

"You made a choice. The Terridae wanted children and, losing the initial drive, became apathetic. Zabul was designed to be moved—why else but in order to search for Earth?"

"The Event will happen," she said uncertainly. "That is what we believe."

"It will happen," he promised. "I'm going to see that it does. But I can't do it alone. And it must be done fast."

"I know Volodya said that, but he will be reasonable. The committee will see to that. He—"

"I'm not talking of Volodya."

"What then?" Her eyes widened. "The Cyclan? But Lim is dead. You destroyed the *Saito*."

Dumarest leaned back, closing his eyes, seeing again the white gush of searing flame from the pyre his bomb had created, which had destroyed the cyber and reduced the ship to a cloud of expanding, incandescent vapor. That battle was won, but the war continued and he knew the forces of the Cyclan must be on their way.

When would they arrive?

Too much time had been wasted while Volodya had made up his mind to throw his weight on the winning side. There had been too many arguments, manipulations, indecisions. The dead weight of inertia had forced him to move slowly when every nerve had screamed for haste. The young had needed to be convinced, their support assured. The Council had to be weakened by subtle innuendo. A dreaming race had to be shaken into wakeful acceptance of the imminence of their destiny.

The work had sapped his stamina and clogged his mind with fatigue and toxins, which introduced the danger of a careless tongue—already he had made one slip which the woman had seemed to ignore. How many others had escaped him due to impatience and frustration?

A balancing act, he thought, feeling himself sink deeper into a semi-doze. To push and yet to appear to be only a reluctant follower. To urge and suggest and persuade and never, ever, to appear more than helpful. As a stranger he would be resented despite open denials. Those who would accept promises and glittering images of the splendid future about to come would gibe at the work necessary to achieve it.

Dreamers—he was trapped in a world of dreamers. Easy prey for the Cyclan when they came unless, first, he could form his own defenses. If Volodya would allow him to. Unless the newly formed committee grew too fond of personal authority.

But that was a knife edge he had to walk if he was ever to find Earth.

CHAPTER THREE

Each day now on waking Vera Jamil spent longer on her toilette, painstakingly arranging her hair, adorning her eyes with touches of cosmetics, adding extra perfume to her bath. These small acts held their own excitement as did the selection and arranging of her clothing. Vanity, of course, but it gave her pleasure and, at times, brought back memories of her youth when Amrik had been alive and they had found magic in the shadowed compartments of Zabul.

A time long gone now yet still she could feel the pain when learning of his death. Still see the smile on his face when they had lifted him from the casket. If nothing else his dreams had been pleasant and she wondered if they had been of her. That was a bad time and she had longed to return to the surcease of forgetfulness, resenting the obligatory periods of wakeful activity. What need did she have of physical stimulation? Of renewing contacts with reality? Amrik was gone and with him had gone her happiness.

Now a small part of it had returned.

It was everywhere in the only world she had ever known; the stir and bustle of expectation, of activity directed to a definite object. Time seemed to have gained a new dimension and she felt the pulse of her blood and the tingle of renewed interest. Luck, she thought; at any other time she would have missed the participation she now enjoyed. Missed the close association with the stranger who had created the new conditions.

"Earl!" She rose as he entered the chamber and turned to him, hands extended, palms upward, smiling her pleasure as he touched them with his own. "I was beginning to think you had forgotten me."

He returned her coquetry with a smile. "Sorry, Vera, but I've been busy."

"I know." Her gesture embraced the shelves, the racks and files and books, the computer data banks of the installation in her charge. "I've been compiling your activities for posterity."

She was too eager but Dumarest retained his smile. Vera Jamil was the custodian of the Archives and could help him ferret out the secrets he hoped they contained. Now, as she produced a pot of steaming tisane together with the traditional cakes of hospitality, he forced himself to mask his impatience.

"Some of the young men were talking of your training program," she said, handing him a cup of the scented tisane. "They admire you even while nursing their bruises. Do men really have to fight like that on other worlds?"

"At times, yes."

"It seems unnatural." Vapor wreathed her eyes as she stared at him over the rim of her cup. "To fight and hurt and maybe to kill. Why can't everyone live in peace?"

"Because all worlds are not like this one." Dumarest set aside the cup and ate a cake. It was good and he said so. "Did you bake it?"

Her flush gave the answer. "An old recipe. Amrik—a friend, used to like them."

"A wise man." Dumarest caught the shadow which drifted over her face and knew better than to labor the point. "Dare I ask if we've made any progress?"

Again the flush, this time caused by his use of words. How nice of him to make her feel an equal partner!

"A little," she said. "There is so much data and you did say to check it all. Give me a moment and we'll get down to business."

She rose to clear away the tisane and cakes, a tall, slender woman, delicately fashioned, her hair a mass of convoluted strands. Hair so blond as to appear almost silver, rising high in an elaborate coiffure, set with small gems which shone like trapped stars. Her face held the ageless placidity of all the

Terridae; she could have been five years older than himself or as many centuries. But, in the real experience of living, she was little more than a child.

"Here is a summary of all references together with computerized assessment. Here is a condensation which negates all duplication. This is a compilation of personal notations; items from old logs and navigational tables together with data from personal journals." She looked at the piled sheaves. "I'm afraid it's rather a lot."

An understatement; the data was indigestible in sheer volume. Dumarest selected a file and ran his eyes over the neat columns of references. The woman had done a thorough job but had missed the point of his search.

He said patiently, "What I hoped for was actual coordinates."

"We have them." She picked up a folder. "The exact location of more than a hundred worlds each of special significance to the Terridae." She added, regretfully, "I'm afraid there's no way of telling which is Earth."

"But surely there are references? Even if the data was coded there must be a key." He saw by her expression that she didn't understand. "Think," he said. "At the beginning the Terridae must have had some information as to the whereabouts of Earth. They would have wanted to safeguard it, perhaps, and what better way than by including it within a framework of dogma? Statements which hold an inner meaning once you know the key." He sought for an example and found it in the creed of the Original People of whom she must know. "Listen," he said, and his voice took on the muted pulse of drums. "From terror they fled to find new places on which to expiate their sins. Only when cleansed will the race of Man be again united."

"Earl?"

"From terror," he said. "That could mean 'From Terra.' Do you see what I'm driving at?"

She said, uncertainly, "Yes, I think so. It's like a riddle, but—" She broke off with a helpless gesture. "I don't know how to solve it."

A failure, but she wasn't wholly to blame. Information retrieval was a skill in itself and one she'd had no reason to develop. Dumarest looked at the files and picked one at random. A listing of data culled from ancient logs including the names of crewmen, cargoes carried, planets visited. Trivia which the Terridae held of value because it had associations with their past. Given time and dedication he would be able to discover their origins, the reason for their withdrawal from normal planetary congress, the ideals which had led them to the formation of their dream. The Event. The finding of Earth.

And he had promised to lead them.

He set down the file, conscious of the woman's stare. How long before she guessed his ignorance? How long before Volodya lost his patience? Pressures to add to the rest but ones he must ignore for the present. As he must gain the help Vera Jamil could give.

He said, smiling, "You've done wonderfully, Vera. I'm just a little stunned at all the information you've managed to accumulate. Now we have to boil it down even further to basic essentials."

"Refine it, you mean?"

"In a way, yes."

"But, Earl, if we knew where Earth was we would have gone there long ago."

The obvious, but he had an answer. "When the location was discovered the time needn't have been right. Details would need to be attended to, arrangements made, things like that. There could have been external pressures which forced a postponement. Then, as time passed, the location could have been forgotten."

"Lost?"

"No, forgotton. Haven't you ever had anything of value which you set to one side for safekeeping then had trouble remembering where you put it? Most of us have had that experience at times. That could have happened to what we're looking for now and our job is to find where it could be. The location of Earth, I mean."

It was hard to remember that she was a grown woman and not a child. Harder still to retain his equanimity when she said, "But you have the answer, Earl. Does it matter if we can't find the location in the Archives?"

"We need confirmation," he said quickly. "Earth lies in a region bounded by the patch of dust lying to the galactic north of Silus, the energy pool known as Morgan's Sink to the galactic west of Crom, and the Hygenium Vortex. Run that area through your computer and determine if any of the planets mentioned fall within those parameters."

Looking at the files she had accumulated, the product of so much labor, she said, "Earl, I'm sorry."

"For what? Trying so hard?" Reaching out he rested the tips of his fingers on the crest of her hair. "I didn't think you'd have the confirmation waiting for me. As you said, if you had the location, you'd be there now. But we'll find it, Vera. Together we'll find it."

Dumarest felt the touch and woke, instantly alert, one hand moving to snatch up his knife and to rest the point against the throat of the woman at his side.

"Earl!" Althea Hesford cringed from the threat. "Earl, for God's sake!"

"I'm sorry." Dumarest set aside the blade, looking at the woman in the pale glow illuminating the room. A nacreous shine emulated the light from a legendary moon. In it the copper sheen of her hair looked darker than it was. "You touched me," he explained. "Startled me. I just reacted."

"I only wanted to see if you were awake."

"Why?"

"To talk." She sat upright in the bed, the soft glow giving her naked flesh a silver sheen. "I couldn't sleep and you felt like a coiled spring lying beside me. You're too tense, Earl. You could have killed me just then. In a week or two, unless you ease the pressure, that could happen. Not deliberately, I'm not saying that, but by simple reflex action."

She was wrong but he didn't argue. "So?"

"You need to relax. If you don't want to take drugs then why not settle for a period of rest in a casket?"

Advice well-meant but he wasn't going to take it. "I haven't the time for that."

"You could find it. You don't have to do everything yourself. You could delegate your authority."

"And what the hell does that mean?" As she made no answer he said, more quietly, "It means you rely on others to do your work. If that is a mark of efficiency then they must follow your example and do the same. In the end you wind up with everyone delegating everything to everyone else and no one doing the actual work."

"It needn't be like that."

"No, but that's the way it happens. You should know. Once you handed authority to the Council what happened? What always happens when you delegate authority to someone else. They hung on to it. It took a near-revolution to make them yield."

To resign and hand over to others who would follow the same path—something he didn't mention. Instead he said, "Is that why you woke me? To tell me I need to rest?"

"No! I—" Then her own tension broke and she laughed. "Put like that it sounds insane. I'm sorry, darling, I guess it's because I've something on my mind."

"Such as?"

"Vera Jamil. You know she's in love with you?"

"Is she?"

"She is and you must know it. And she isn't the only one. Earl! I'm jealous!"

"Of Vera?" Deliberately he kept his tone casual. "I need her help, Althea, and if a few kind words will get it then that's what I'll give. But she isn't in love with me. She's enamored of change. She's waking up as others are and realizing what life can be all about."

"Pain," she said quietly. "Hurt. Fear. Anger. Envy. Frustration. Rejection—you want me to go on?"

"Life," he said. "It was never intended to be easy."

"I know. You told me, life is a continual act of violence." She leaned forward to hug her knees, the mane of her hair veiling her face, the curves of her torso. "You seem to believe that."

"The spermatozoon which fertilized the egg from which you sprang fought against a billion others for the privilege. The antibiotics in your body battle endlessly against invading bacteria. Your brain was developed because you enjoyed a high-protein diet. Each mouthful of food comes from the dead. Life is what it is, woman, not what you'd like it to be."

And he was suited to live it better than anyone she knew. To fight and kill in order to survive—how many others in Zabul could do the same? Even Volodya was strong only in relation to those around him. How to hold such a man? To keep him close so as to shelter beneath his protection?

She felt the urgings of her body and was shaken by the sudden realization of the power of nature's dominance. Was this how a primitive woman had chosen her mate? Giving herself to the strongest so as to gain his favor? Bearing his children? Continuing his line?

She said, "There's been talk, Earl. Discussion leading to argument about how you intend leading us all to the Event. Some think you plan to shift Zabul but we know that isn't possible."

"So?"

"They want to know, Earl. The committee and others. They have the right."

"When the time comes they will."

"Some think the time is now."

"And others?" He provided the answer. "How many are beginning to think it would be better not to go at all?"

"A few," she admitted. "And their numbers are growing. You can't blame them, Earl. They are old and afraid and see no reason to change. And others are willing to wait a little longer."

"You?"

"I'm not sure," she said slowly. "Up until now it was easy to long for the Event. It was so remote it didn't matter. But now you've made it immediate and people are beginning to have second thoughts. Some people," she added. "And, yes, you could include me among them."

"Life," he said. "You're afraid of life."

"Afraid of what it could bring," she corrected. "After we reach Earth—what then?"

Change and that was fearsome enough to those born and bred in a static society. The need to make constant decisions. The fear that, perhaps, the fabled world wasn't as claimed. Doubt and the terror of insecurity. The need to grow from child into an adult.

"Earl? Don't you understand? I'm afraid of losing you."

He turned away from her, aware of her nearness, the radiated femininity of her body. Rising, he headed toward the shower, there to let ice-cold water drum on his head and over his body. Stung with chill he dried himself and returned to the bedroom to see the woman still hunched as he had left her. Even as he watched the light changed to simulate a dawn.

It grew from the walls, the ceiling, a warm suffusion of red and gold, amber and orange, pink and russet. A birth which turned the room into a miniature world and the woman into a thing of flame. Hair, skin, mouth, nails, the membrane within her nostrils and beyond her parted lips—all warm and redolent of summer heat.

"Earl!" She leaned back lifting her arms toward him. "Earl, my darling! Earl!"

Then her arms were around him, the heat of her passion filling his world.

The uniform was grey, fashioned after his own clothing; the blouse long-sleeved, close at the wrists and the collar high around the neck, the pants thrust into knee-high boots. The armband bore the device of a quartered circle.

"The symbol of Earth," explained Erik Medwin. "What do you think, Commander?"

Dumarest said, "I've been promoted?"

"You're the boss as far as we're concerned. The man we intend to follow. What do you think of the uniform?"

Medwin stood still as Dumarest examined it. The material was fabric coated with flexible plastic, giving some protection but nothing like the metal mesh buried within his own. The cut could be improved and red chafe-marks showed at the young man's neck.

"Who made it up?"

"Giselda Mapron and her friends. This is a sample and it'll be altered if needed. I just wanted to show you and get your approval. Will it do, Commander?"

"With adjustments, yes. Remember a uniform is something you may have to fight in so it must be comfortable as well as tough. That collar's too tight; when you fight your neck will swell and you don't want to choke yourself. Make it looser here and here." Dumarest touched the neck and chest. "Stiffen the material over the shoulders and include protective plates if you can. They'll prevent a broken clavicle if anyone comes at you with a club and strikes the shoulder. Stiffen the boots too—a kick in the shin can cripple a man if he isn't protected. The same for the groin. And you'll need a hat of some kind, but make it strong enough to withstand a blow. One with a face-visor would be best."

"To protect the eyes," said Medwin. "I hadn't thought of that. Volodya's guards don't wear them."

"They aren't going where we are."

"True," mused Medwin. "And how can you salute without a hat? How about insignia of rank?"

"Learn about that from where you learned about saluting," said Dumarest. "And remember to thank Vera Jamil for her trouble."

"You know?"

"Where else would you get the information?" Dumarest smiled to soften his comment. "How are you getting on?"

"The first class are now instructing and we've tripled the intake. A mixed batch, the girls insisted on joining in on equal terms."

"Training?"

"Basic. Synchronized movement with practice using knives and staves. Unarmed combat too." He added, "We've had some injuries but the medics have taken care of them."

"And you've been to see them?"

Medwin hesitated. "Well, what with one thing and another, I guess I've been too busy."

"A leader must take care of his men," said Dumarest. "If he wants authority without responsibility then he isn't worthy of his command. Remember that. The people you train now could save your life later on. If you treat them like dirt they may not be too eager to do that. Those injured people got hurt because they tried to please you. Let's go and see how they're getting on."

A medic met them as they entered the ward, lifting his eyebrows at the sight of Medwin in his new uniform, turning to Dumarest as if knowing he was the leader of the pair. He frowned as he heard the request.

"See them? All eleven?"

"If you can arrange it. Are they badly hurt?"

"Broken bones, a lost eye, two with punctured lungs, one with a smashed kneecap, another with a ruptured spleen." He added dryly, "Your new ideals seem to encourage the young to be violent."

They lay in a small room, bandaged, some in traction. All were conscious, even the one who had lost an eye. He waved as Dumarest entered followed by Medwin.

"You've come to see us? Well, what about that! Did you hear what happened to me?"

"You lost an eye," said Dumarest. "In combat that makes you a liability. Are they giving you a new one?"

"Sure. It's growing now. In a few days I'll be as good as new."

As would they all. Zabul didn't lack for trained doctors and expensive drugs; slow time alone would promote quick healing, the metabolism accelerated to turn seconds into hours. Sedated, fed by intravenous injection, the most badly injured would wake healed if hungry.

Dumarest led the way down the line, speaking to each in turn, waiting as Medwin did the same. Back at the door he turned and lifted an arm in a farewell salute.

"You've done well," he said. "All of you. You've shown courage and you've accepted your misfortune. But I hope you've learned from it. Like I said earlier, an injury makes a combat soldier a liability. In actual conflict some of you would have had to be abandoned. Just remember that the next time you want to take a chance—sometimes the odds aren't worth it."

As they neared the exit Dumarest said, "You go ahead, Erik. Get those uniforms adapted as I suggested. And we want no more injuries, understand?"

"Yes, Commander!"

"Off you go then."

Dumarest returned the vague salute and went in search of the infirmary's biological technician. The man was in his laboratory, his face intent, as he examined the projected image of a slide.

"From one of the young fools who tried to get themselves killed," he explained. "An unsuspected infection which must be dealt with."

"A mutation?"

Sneh Thorne nodded. He was a round man with a face normally placid but now creased in lines of concentration.

"It could well be that. I'm trying a wide range of antibiotics so as to effect a cure without recourse to surgery but if the infection becomes too widespread we'll have to remove the affected area and grow a replacement from uncontaminated tissue." He snapped off the projection and straightened, easing his back. "What we really need, of course, is a general-purpose antibiotic which will destroy all objects foreign to the basic DNA cellular imprint."

"Coupled with a regenerative agent to replace all damaged and missing tissue to the same plan?"

"It would save all doctors a hell of a lot of work," admitted Thorne. "In fact it could almost put us out of business. A man gets hurt and he crawls into a corner somewhere to eat and sleep while his body repairs itself. No scar tissue, no maladjusted bone structure. No areas of fibroid encystment. An eye, an arm, a leg or an internal organ all regenerating to match the basic pattern. If the liver can do it why not other organs? And what, for example, has a lobster got that we haven't? A creature like that can regrow a claw but we can't even regenerate a finger."

"We aren't lobsters," reminded Dumarest,

"No, sometimes I think we're a damned sight worse. What other creature would deliberately set out to injure itself? Those fools in the ward have given us more work than we've known for the past century. And that isn't counting the scrapes and bruises and minor lacerations. The strains and minor hemorrhages and psychic damage. You're a menace, Earl. As much a danger to our society as that damned bacteria!"

"Which by its presence is triggering the body to manufacture a defense."

"True." Thorne ran a hand over his rumpled hair. "I guess I'm just tired. Life goes on and on and nothing ever seemed to happen and then, suddenly, I'm faced with challenges."

Dumarest said, "That's what makes life exciting. Did you manage to do as I asked?"

"Another challenge."

"Did you?"

"It's in the small laboratory," said Thorne reluctantly. "Everything you asked for, but God knows what you intend doing with it." Pausing, he added, "Are you certain you can manage alone?"

"I'll make out."

"If you need assistance I'll be willing to help." Thorne looked hopefully at Dumarest then sighed as he recognized the other's determination. "No? Well, as you want. I guess it's your business. I'll show you the way."

The place was small but well-equipped. Alone, Dumarest examined the gleaming apparatus, the vials and containers, the microscopes and manipulative devices. Things which hypno-tuition had taught him to use. Materials and knowledge which could save his life.

CHAPTER FOUR

Brandt had gone, leaving behind the acrid scent of her perfume, accentuated by the exudations of age, but she had been reasonable and had taken little prompting to recognize the danger. Lijert too had been swayed after some discussion but he, like the woman, had been old and already uneasily aware of the passage of time. Days and weeks edged into months, eating at their reserves, lopping years from their anticipated life-spans. Brandt and Lijert were two of the committee who would back him without argument and he felt Stanton could be another, for he was a man who resented the disturbance of old patterns despite his relative youth. He had found the burden of responsibility more irksome than he'd guessed, not even suspecting that the tiresome routine beneath which he chafed had been deliberately imposed.

Who else would help him to take over sole command?

Urick Volodya pondered this problem as he crossed the room to stand looking down at the men set in a neat array on the chessboard resting on a table fashioned of convoluted woods inlaid with metallic ornamentation.

Towitsch? Prideaux? The girl was a fanatic and her opposite number little better, but if a wedge could be driven between them it was possible one would vote from reasons of malice rather than from calculated decision. Did Towitsch love Dumarest? A possibility and one holding promise. If so she could let jealousy turn her against Hesford. But what of Prideaux?

Reaching down, Volodya moved the pieces in the opening

39

moves of an established game. How easy it would be if people could be manipulated like the pieces on the board? And yet did he need to feel such concern? The old ways had gone and now was the time of opportunity. He had recognized it and made his move. It was but one further step to the consolidation of his power.

Why worry about pawns?

The men scattered beneath the sweep of his hand and he turned to pace the floor, tall, arrogant, his hooded eyes and beaked nose giving him the look of an imperious bird of prey, Dumarest noted when, ushered by guards, he stepped into the room.

It was large, a chamber chosen to reflect the personality of its occupant, and he looked at the soft coverings on the floor, the ornate furniture, the scattered chessmen lying in gold and silver disarray.

"Earl!" Volodya stepped forward, smiling, hands extended in the traditional gesture. "You will have wine? Some cakes? The formalities need to be observed. And a chair—there is no need for you to stand. All I want to do is talk. We have reason for a discussion, I think. You agree?"

"Haven't you been kept informed of progress?"

"I've had reports." Volodya lost his smile. "But from you hardly a word. I think it time we rectified the matter. Come! Have some wine!"

He poured and handed Dumarest a goblet of silver chased with gold. The wine itself was sweet with a rich body and an aftertaste of mint.

Dumarest sipped then said, "I see you've a liking for chess."

"Yes. Do you play?"

"I know the game. Some claim it to be a symbolic battle and say those who play good chess will make good commanders in time of war." He added dryly, "Those who think that have never experienced a field of conflict."

"We know little of war."

"And power?" Dumarest took another sip of his wine. "Certain things seem to be universal. The love of authority, for example. Couple it with a lack of responsibility and you have a lure few can resist. Of course, it has its dangers."

"Such as?"

"Rebellion. Assassination." Dumarest ate a cake. "The fruit

of defiance, disobedience and distrust. Dangers a wise ruler avoids."

A warning? Dumarest was more subtle than he seemed and, Volodya guessed, far more devious than he appeared. To underestimate him could be the worst mistake he would ever make. The worst and, perhaps, the last.

"How is your nephew getting on?" Dumarest was casual. "Alva Kirek, the one in the Earth Corps."

"Well enough. He seems to be happy with the uniform."

"It gives them a sense of comradeship."

"As does the name?"

"It wasn't of my choosing," said Dumarest. "You know that."

As he knew other things. "The laboratory," he demanded. "Why did you want it?"

Dumarest remained silent.

"Then let us talk of Vera Jamil." Volodya poured them each a little more wine. "As yet, I understand, you have had no success."

"Corroboration? No."

"Of course. You must know where Earth lies—or how could you promise to lead us to it?" Volodya leaned forward in his chair. "You *do* know?"

"I never said that."

"No. You were born on Earth and stowed away on a strange ship when young and later were abandoned to make your own way on planets which knew nothing of your home world. But you want to return, which is what brought you to Zabul." Volodya tasted his wine and sat holding the goblet. Beneath the arch of his brows his eyes were brightly direct. "You think we have the answer?"

"Have you?"

"No." Volodya set down his goblet and seemed, abruptly, to relax. "Or if we have it is a mystery yet to be solved. The Archives are, as you have learned, basically a mass of useless trivia. What else can you expect? So little happens here that all small details gain in importance so we have lists of births and deaths and petty quarrels. Details of stores and minutes of meetings and deliberations of the Councils with comment on decisions made."

"Then why maintain the Archives?"

"Habit," said Volodya. "Tradition and something more.

The Terridae spend their lives mostly in dreams and have little time for learning. The Archives form a repository of knowledge—how else would our technical staff learn their skills? And each culture should have a history. Roots which hold them firm in the path they have chosen to follow. Signs to give the direction to take. With us it is the Event. The hope of finding Earth and the wonders it has to give. And yet, if we did—what then?"

A question which held familiar echoes. Althea had posed it—how many others?

Dumarest said, "You are telling me you believe it better to travel than to arrive."

"For some, yes. For the Terridae, certainly."

A confession and Dumarest wondered why Volodya had made it. The room gave the answer as did the scattered chessmen lying on the floor.

He said, "From the beginning you have been playing a part. Using me for your own purposes."

"Of course. Does that annoy you?" Volodya shrugged. "How else to break the impasse I faced? The Council was old and determined to cling to power. I had no support and no reason for any direct action. You provided them both. It was expedient to pretend to believe you while altering the balance of power. To back you and so gain the adherence of those to whom you were a hero. Once the Council was deposed it was still politic to give you open support. I wanted to avoid all danger of being accused of betrayal. Failure, when it came, had to originate with you."

"You were certain I would fail?"

"It was only a matter of giving you enough time."

"And now?"

"You have had enough time."

"I see." Dumarest rose and crossed the room to where the scattered chessmen lay bright against the carpet. He picked them up, set them in place on the board and, without looking at Volodya, said, "You had it all worked out from the beginning, didn't you? Move after move just like a game of chess. Forcing others to move as you wanted. But you forget something." He turned to face the other man, his face as cold and as hard as the pieces on the board. "Others can play the same game."

"You?"

"Yes," said Dumarest. "Me."

The wine was forgotten, the cakes, the small pretenses which had masked savage determinations. Volodya and Dumarest faced each other like opponents in a ring. Fighters armed with weapons more complex than knives.

"The Corps," said Volodya. "That gang of thugs you've taught to fight. Do you think them a match for my guards?"

"They don't have to be."

"Then—"

"A mistake," said Dumarest. "One of your first. You permitted the formation of the Corps, but you had no real choice. To deny the young a chance to prepare themselves for the Event would be to admit you didn't think it would happen. But you instructed your nephew to join so as to keep you informed. Another mistake; he grew to like his new companions."

"The badge," said Volodya bitterly. "The uniform. The rank. The drill."

"Bait," said Dumarest. "Empires have been founded with less."

"As you would know. What other errors did I make?"

"You underestimated the power of a dream. You still underestimate it. Probably because your own was small. You wanted to become the ruler of Zabul and you've achieved that ambition. The committee is a farce and we both know it. It may amuse you to manipulate the members but they are a facade to maintain a pretense of democratic function. If you hadn't realized that then you are less shrewd than I thought. But others have more ambition than to lord it over a tiny, artificial world. They want what the galaxy can give them. They want Earth!"

As he wanted it; the need blazed from his face, his eyes. Volodya had never seen that yearning before and, for a moment, he was awed by its sheer intensity—the need and the determination to achieve it.

"I've promised them the Event," said Dumarest. "Do you want me to tell them you deny it? Can you imagine what they will do?"

"I can handle any insurrection."

"How? By stationing a guard at each terminal? On every

junction and staging point? In every installation? How many would you need? And how can you force people to tend the hydroponic farms and maintain air and power?"

"That threat was used before," said Volodya coldly. "It suited me to persuade the Council to yield to it, but now things are not the same. While I rule in Zabul there will be no defiance. To give in to force is to surrender to the mob. Do you advocate anarchy?"

"Not here."

"I'm glad to hear it. At least we agree on that. And don't imagine the situation you postulate would be allowed to continue. The old outnumber the young and are aware of the need of discipline if the environment is to be maintained. As were the original builders."

They had incorporated pipes to convey paralyzing gas to each essential installation, a precaution, as were the airtight doors, the monitoring alarms, the scanners set throughout the complex of passages and rooms. These details Dumarest had learned from his study of the plans.

He said, "Wires can be cut, pipes blocked, doors jammed."

Volodya brushed this aside. "None of the Terridae would do such a thing. It is a measure of your desperation that you even mention it."

"Yes," said Dumarest. "A good word. But a desperate man can be dangerous. Tell me, if a ship of the Cyclan were to appear and demand I be handed over to them what would you do?"

"That depends."

"On whether or not they threatened harm to Zabul? Supposing they did. Supposing any ship came with the same threat and the same demand. Would you defy them?"

"Would you expect me to?"

"No. That is why I had to make sure it wouldn't happen. Why you wouldn't have the choice." A phone rested on a small table against a wall. Dumarest crossed to it, picked up the handset and looked at Volodya. "A demonstration," he said. "Just to show you how wrong a man can be." To the instrument he snapped, "Captain Medwin! Immediately." A pause, then, "Operation Five. Commence!"

The phone made a small click as he replaced it in its cradle. Nothing had changed and yet Volodya felt the tension. A knotting of the stomach and an impression as if he stood on the edge of a chasm. Bluff, it had to be a bluff, what could Dumarest do?

But why bluff if it was to be so quickly proven an empty threat?

"What do you want?"

"Wait," said Dumarest.

The man was sweating despite his outward calm. The threat of sabotage, despite his swift rejection, had made an effect. Volodya was a product of his environment. To him as to all the Terridae the safety of Zabul was paramount. The weakness which made them vulnerable to any demand.

"Soon," said Dumarest. "Now!"

It was nothing, the barest flicker of the lights, but it was enough to send Volodya racing to slam his hand against a button.

"Guards! To me! Guards!"

The flicker quickened as men burst through the door. Young, strong, wearing pants and shirts of dull olive, each bearing a club, each armed with a gun capable of spouting a cloud of stunning gas. These were short-range weapons but effective enough in limited areas and without the danger of missile-guns or lasers. Two of them ran to flank Dumarest where he stood, another staying at the door, the fourth halting before Volodya.

"Sir?"

"Hold him." Volodya gestured toward Dumarest. "Stun him if he attempts to move. Send to the generators and see what is going on. Halt all movement and—"

"Why waste time?" Dumarest glanced at the lights, now flickering faster than before. "And why create a panic? An interrupter mechanism has been placed in the wiring and will continue to function for another few minutes. It was activated by my order as you heard. Unless I rescind it the interrupter will fuse at the end of its cycle and burn out half a mile of conduit. Nothing serious—but other devices could be. What do you want to do?"

A bluff, Volodya was sure of it, but the risk was too great to take a chance. The flickering was bad enough—anything interrupting the smooth flow of life in Zabul was cause for alarm. And if irritation should pile on irritation he could guess what would happen.

"I yield," he snapped. Then, to the guards, "Leave us!" At least it had been his men who had answered his summons. To Dumarest he said, "Am I to beg?"

"No." Dumarest reached the phone, spoke, put it down. As the flickering halted he said, "All I want from you is one thing. I want to talk to a previous custodian of the Archives. The oldest one you have."

Down in the deepest levels the air was chill, echoes muffled by absorbent padding, the light a dull, bluish glow. Resting in low-roofed compartments separated by thick walls the caskets of the Terridae stood like massive sarcophagi. The boxes were carved and ornamented with a host of figures and mystic symbols—abstract designs which held esoteric meaning, among them the signs of the zodiac.

This was the clue which had brought him to Zabul and now Dumarest waited as a technician worked at one of the caskets.

"We must give him time," said Althea Hesford, as if guessing at his impatience. "Shiro Gourvich is a very old man."

Gourvich even now was lost in a world of entrancing dreams as he lay in the snug confines of his casket, experiencing illusions created by mental stimulation as his drugged body lay in the surrogate womb. For him time had been extended, his metabolism slowed, bodily functions served by sophisticated machinery. The box itself formed a miniature world, airtight, strong, containing its own power source and essential supplies. A fortress against the ravages of time.

"How much longer?" Dumarest looked at the technician. The box could only be opened from within either by intent or by time-lapse mechanisms unless special techniques were applied.

"He's old," said the man, echoing Althea. "And frail. If you want him alive you've got to give him time. I've triggered the operation and I guess he's coming out of it about now. A few more minutes and—" He grunted as the lid of the casket began to rise. "I was wrong. He's awake now. You want me around?"

He left as Dumarest shook his head. The lid of the casket, now opened, revealed a padded interior and the frame and face of an old man within.

An *old* man.

Old!

The sparse white hair was like gossamer, the face a canvas for endless lines, the mouth a bloodless slit, the eyes twin balls of flawed glass set deep within sunken sockets. The body itself, beneath a simple robe, was a thing of twigs and sticks and stringy muscle. The voice was like the rustle of leaves in early winter.

"Has it happened? The Event. Has it come?"

"Not yet." Althea was gentle. "How do you feel? Can you sit upright?"

"Of course." Gourvich reared to clutch at the lowered side of the casket with bird-claw hands. "I'm a little vague, that's all. I was young, you see, and Lynne was with me. There was a rolling meadow over which we ran and a lake and then beds of flowers in which we made endless love. Why did you wake me? I have the right to rest undisturbed until the coming of the Event. But you say it has not arrived."

Dumarest said, "I need your help."

"Help? What help can I give you, young man? The strength of my arm?" The chuckle was as dry as the voice. "A fly could break it. My skills? They are forgotten. My influence with the Council? It ended when they deemed me too old to face the routine wakenings. What can you want from me?"

"Your memories."

"Of what? Lynne? Hilda? Others I have known?"

"Your memory and your skill," said Dumarest patiently. He knew the shock of resurrection—the old man was bearing it well. "Zabul needs your help."

"Zabul? Are we in danger?"

"No," said Althea quickly. "It is a problem which needs to be solved and you are the best fitted to do it. Can you rise? Do you need a stimulant?"

"A little help." The old man sagged in her supporting arms. "It has been a long time, I think. Who now heads the Council?"

"Urich Volodya."

"Volodya? Do I remember him?" The brow moved to change the pattern of creases, the eyes narrowing with the frown. "Sergi?"

"Urich. Sergi was his father."

"I knew him when he was a boy. And you, my dear?"

Gourvich looked at Althea. "No. No, I don't remember you at all."

She had probably been born after he had entered the casket as had Urich Volodya and how many others. Dumarest looked at the old man as he stood sipping the cordial Althea had brought with her, a heavy syrup containing strength-giving drugs to sharpen the mind and speed the slowed processes of the body. The chemicals would rob Gourvich of extended years but enable him to stiffen a little, to look more alert, to shake off some of the vagueness which had clothed him in the shedded webs of time.

Years, decades, centuries, millennia—how old could he be?

The young were needed to maintain Zabul and denied use of the caskets until they had reached thirty. Then they were permitted only intermittent use, woken at frequent intervals to maintain physical prowess and contact with reality. These periods lessened as they grew older, ceasing when, like Gourvich, they had nothing to offer the community.

A thousand years?

More?

It was possible—quick time reduced hours to seconds and the drugs used were more sophisticated, compounds which voyaging. Even allowing for a reduced efficiency and frequent wakings, Gourvich could be well over a thousand years old. Time enough for tissues to shrink and unused muscle to avoided the inherent dangers of those used during normal wither. Time, too, for memories to fade.

Dumarest considered this as he followed Althea and her charge to the elevator and up to the Archives where Vera Jamil was waiting. He caught her expression and recognized her resentment and jealousy and smiled as he guided the old man into a chair.

"We need your help, Vera, and I'm sure you won't refuse it. This is Shiro Gourvich. An early custodian. Shiro, this is Vera Jamil, your successor. If you ask her nicely she will make you some of her special tisane."

"With althenus?"

"I prefer fredich," she said. "It has more flavor, but I'll make it with althenus if you want."

"He wants," said Dumarest. "And I'd like to taste it too." He saw her warm beneath his smile, as, turning to Althea, he said, "You've done well. Perhaps you'd like to tell Urich of our progress? He's probably waiting for your report."

He wanted her out of the way and she knew why. Knew too that if she objected he would insist and so add to the other woman's pleasure. But why did he have to pander to her? To order, surely, was enough.

An error Dumarest did not make. He had noted the extra perfume Vera was wearing, her eyes when she had seen him with Althea. Did she resent the rival or imagine herself to be slighted? It would take so little to negate his search for what he needed.

Now he said to Gourvich, "Vera has performed a miracle in condensing the appropriate data in the Archives but something is missing and we need your help to find it. But first the tisane." He waited until it had been served and tasted. "Good?"

"Very good." Gourvich inhaled the vapor rising from the cup and took another sip. "Lynne used to make it like this. Did I tell you about Lynne? She and I burned in a mutual passion and—well, you know what it is to be young."

And were learning what it was to be old and approaching senility. Life could be extended but even with the mental stimulus provided the glands grew out of synchronization with the rest of the body, thoughts jumped wider gaps, made new neuron paths in the cortex. The line between fact and fantasy grew blurred and time became impacted so the memory of childhood became stronger than that of yesterday.

Gourvich seemed to be aware of this. He said quietly, "I am not what I was. If this were the Event I should bathe in magic pools and become young again, but you woke me too early. I do not thank you for that. The price of this tisane could be my immortality."

"We didn't mean—"

"No!" Dumarest cut the woman short. "No apologies. We offer you the Event and soon. The next time you wake could be on Earth."

The old man savored that promise as if it were air, sucking it deep into his lungs, holding it, releasing it with a regretful sigh.

"Could," he murmured. "You express a doubt."

"One you can resolve." Dumarest waited as Gourvich

sipped more tisane. "When you were young Earth must have been very close. The Event was to happen soon. Am I right?"

"There were difficulties," said Gourvich. "Expenses. Things had to be settled before the search could begin. It was decided to wait a little."

The delay had stretched on the grounds of expediency and compromise. The urgency forgotten in a mass of petty detail. Slowed by those in authority who had been reluctant to disturb the status quo.

Dumarest explained this as if to a child, Gourvich nodding his agreement.

"You could be right," he said. "I cannot remember now. There were arguments and passions and insults and, once, a killing. It is all in the Archives." He looked at the woman. "In data bank 153/239. Or is it 235/879? Or did the Council decide to expunge the record?" He looked at his cup. "This is very good tisane."

"Would you like some more?"

"Lynne makes good tisane. You must meet her and try it sometime. Bring your friend." He blinked at Dumarest. "Do I know you?"

"We're old friends," said Dumarest. "And you're going to help me. Now think of the time when you were custodian. I'll bet you knew everything in the Archives. All the data on Earth—you would have to know. When they asked your advice you could give them a calculated report. Details as to the distance to be traveled and the direction. Things like that." He paused to let Gourvich grasp what he was saying. "Earth, Shiro. Think of Earth."

"One day," said Gourvich. "One day we'll find it and when we do we'll find all we could ever hope for. I'll be with Lynne again and Graham and Claude and Hilda. We'll reform the group. Maybe you could join. You and your lady—she makes good tisane."

"It happens," whispered Vera. "Earl, it happens!"

Dumarest looked down at his hand, clenched now into a fist, the knuckles white with strain. He forced himself to ease the fingers, flexing them, conscious of the sweat on his face, the perspiration stinging his eyes. To be so close! So close!

"Degeneration?"

She nodded then explained, "It happens when a person gets too old or has lived too long in dreams. For a while he seems to be rational, then physical stress causes a mental relapse. For him, now, this is just another fantasy. He doesn't know where he is or what you are saying. He might even believe that he's answered your question—if he ever had the answer at all. If it exists here in Zabul."

An entire culture dedicated to the finding of Earth—it was against all logic they had met with nothing but failure. But if they hadn't the entire answer then they must have clues. He could piece together fragments with his own, hard-won information, and that data could give him the coordinates.

"Think!" he said to the old man. "Think, damn you think! Talk to me of Earth. Earth, man! Earth!"

"Earl!"

"Be quiet, woman!" he heard the sharp intake of her breath and realized she thought he might strike the old man with something more solid than words. The fear was groundless but he expressed it as Gourvich stared blankly into his cup. "I won't hurt him. I'm just trying to guide the direction of his thoughts. To do that I must claim his attention. Have you more tisane? Good. Fill his cup. Touch him as you do it. Caress his hair, his cheek, his hand. Anything to make him aware of your presence." As she obeyed, steam rising from the cup, her fingers trailing over the bird-claw of his hand, Dumarest said, "Drink your tisane, Shiro. Lynne made it for you."

"Lynne?"

"She's here. Didn't you feel her touch you? She's waiting for you to tell us about Earth. The floating cities and towers of sparkling crystal. The pools of eternal youth and the mountains clothed in singing rainbows. The plains and seas and the Shining Ones. Far out, you said. Somewhere close to the Rim."

"Did I?"

"That's what you said. A place where the stars are few and the nights dark."

Gourvich shook his head. "Not when there's a moon."

"Of course. The moon. Silver, isn't it? Big. A fit companion for Earth. And you're going to take us there. Show us the way. It's a secret but you can tell Lynne. You love each other." Dumarest's voice became a pulsing susurration holding the hammering impact of a drum. "Tell, Lynne, Shiro.

Tell her about Earth. Tell her. Tell her how to find Earth.
Tell her. Tell her. Tell her, Shiro. Tell her."

On and on as Gourvich stared blankly into his cup.
Dumarest falling silent as, abruptly, the old man lifted his
head.

In a thin, cracked voice, his mouth twisted into a vacuous
grin he chanted, "Thirty-two, forty, sixty-seven—that's the
way to get to heaven. Seventy-nine, sixty, forty-three—are
you following me? Forty-six, seventy, ninety-five—up good
people, live and thrive!"

Madness?

The babblings of a deranged mind?

Dumarest reached forward and touched the old man's
throat. The skin was flaccid, clammy beneath his touch, the
pulse slow, turgid in its barely discoverable beat. The eyes
were closed and spittle ran from the corner of the mouth
tracing a glistening smear over the chin. Pushed too hard he
had withdrawn into a catatonic safety.

"Is he dead, Earl?"

"No. In shock. I made him think of something he pre-
ferred to forget." Rising, Dumarest looked at the woman.
"That chant—have you heard it before? Does it mean anything to you?"

"No." Vera frowned, thinking. "It sounded like a childish
numbers game of some kind. I haven't heard it myself. Maybe if—"

She broke off as her face turned red. Her hair, her clothes,
the entire interior of the Archives were dyed with a flood of
scarlet light as the alarms tore the air with their demanding
clangor.

CHAPTER FIVE

Medwin met Dumarest in the corridor, halting, snapping a salute. "An attack, Commander! Your orders?"

He was keen, eager for action, face glowing with a new vibrancy. His uniform, modified to Dumarest's suggestion, was neat, looking less like a fancy dress than an outfit intended for serious use. The helmet, crested, perforated over the ears, supported a transparent visor, now raised. The belt at his waist supported a yard-long club.

"Commander?"

Dumarest said, "At ease, Captain. Has the attack been verified?"

"As an attack, no," admitted the young man. "But objects have been spotted approaching Zabul."

Which meant Volodya had acted with unnecessary precipitation and Dumarest wondered as to his motive. Althea would have reported the resurrecting of the old custodian—had Volodya been afraid of what he might reveal? The man himself was beyond further questioning and would shortly be back in his casket there, most likely, to dream until he died.

Medwin, impatient, said, "What are your orders, Commander?"

"Place the entire Corps on full combat-alert. Have the trained units stand by for external operation. Once you have made your dispositions let me know. I shall be in Command."

These were orders Medwin wanted to hear. "Do you expect a fight, Commander?"

"I'd prefer to avoid one."

"But—"

"A soldier's job is to fight, is that it?" Dumarest saw the other's nod of agreement. "People get killed in battle," he reminded. "It could be you or me or a mutual friend. A good officer remembers that. The correct way to conduct a fight is to win it with the minimum amount of casualties and damage. Your men expect you to take good care of them and so do I."

"But, sir, what if we can't avoid a fight and can't avoid getting hurt?"

"Then you go in to win and to hell with the cost. Understand?"

"Yes, sir!"

Dumarest returned Medwin's snapped salute and watched him move at a run down the passage before making his way to Command. The flashing red glare and strident noise of the alarm had ended, leaving the passages and halls filled with men and women scurrying like ants blindly racing through a disturbed nest. A false impression; Urich Volodya had imposed a strict discipline of survival, backed by his guards. Two of them, stationed outside the chamber, stared at Dumarest but made no attempt to bar his entrance. Inside, the place hummed with controlled activity.

Technicians sat at their consoles scattered on the large expanse of the floor; observers, environmental monitors, armigers, assessors, predictors. Their faces were touched by the illumination from their instruments, the telltales and registers and dials. Other light came from the huge screens flanking the walls and depicting the universe outside. A glitter of countless stars interspersed and overlaid with sheets and curtains of luminescence, the ebon blotches of clouds of interstellar dust, the fuzz of distant nebulae.

"Earl!" Althea came toward him, face pale against the copper sheen of her hair. She caught his arm as he stepped to where Volodya stood at the main console. "They're coming, Earl. Just as you said they would."

"How many?"

"Seven." Volodya spoke without turning to look at Dumarest. "All heading on a direct collision course with Zabul."

"Seven?"

"Approaching from two different directions."

"Are you sure as to the number?" Dumarest snarled his impatience as Volodya nodded. "Look at me, damn you! Has there been contact?"

"As yet only visual." Volodya touched a control on the bank before him and, on a screen, a familiar object appeared in blurred magnification. "This is approaching from the west and north." The image shrank a little to reveal three other shapes trailing the first. "A group of four. The others are coming from the east and south." The screen flickered, steadying to illustrate the other vessels. They were near-twins of the others.

Ships at which Dumarest stared before he said, "None are under drive. When did you spot them?"

"Just before I sounded the alarm."

Then the ships had dropped from plus-C velocity and could be identified for what they were. Their numbers alone would have jarred Volodya and made him sound the Red Alert. But seven?

Dumarest looked closer at the images on the screen. None of the vessels approaching from the south were wrapped in the blue shimmer of the Erhaft field, which meant they were coasting on gained momentum. At his order Volodya put the other group on a second screen.

"Not one of them is under drive," said Dumarest. "And no contact as yet?"

"No."

"Try again. Use wide-dispersal and include the code used to contact your regular suppliers. Demand a response and don't be polite."

"Right, Commander." A technician didn't wait for Volodya to relay the order. He added, "Captain Medwin reports the Corps is in position."

"Thanks. Can you patch me into a communication circuit?"

"It's done, Commander. Just relay through me."

An unexpected ally and Dumarest wondered if he had others in Command. An armiger gave him a part of the answer, lifting a hand in salute from where he sat at his console. The salute was repeated by an environmental engineer.

To Volodya Dumarest said, "A divided command is the surest recipe for failure. You rule Zabul, but I suggest you allow me to conduct this present operation."

"And if I refuse?" Volodya saw the answer in Dumarest's eyes. "You'd put it to the test, right?"

"It needn't come to that."

"But you'd threaten Zabul if I refuse. What gives you the conviction you can handle this better than I can?"

"You play good chess," said Dumarest. "But you're hopeless at poker. You just can't recognize a bluff."

"I don't understand."

"Look at those ships. Put them on the screens, matched images, full magnification." He waited as Volodya obeyed. Gave the man time to study what he saw. "Well?"

"Ships," said Volodya. "Armed, by the look of them. They could destroy Zabul."

"Decoys," snapped Dumarest. "Use your eyes, man! The lead vessel is real enough but those following are drogues. Inflated bladders bearing metallic paint and equipped with a small guidance device inside. They look real enough and will register on your scanners but they're only balloons."

"Then why use them?"

"Bluff. They can frighten and each one will take an expensive torpedo to destroy. It's a mercenary's trick." Lifting his voice he said, "Any response as yet to our demand for contact?"

"None, Commander."

"Sound battle-alert. All unessential Terridae to take to their caskets. All combat personnel to be suited against exposure to the void. Total closure of all seals."

"At once, Commander!" The environmental engineer busied himself with his console.

"Communications?"

"Commander!"

"Send a final demand for contact. Warn that unless they respond immediately we open fire. Armiger! Aim missiles at both lead ships with contact and remote-controlled warheads. Aim others at the decoys. Have them loaded with thermite flares. Fire them on order." Dumarest waited, counting seconds. "Any response as yet?"

"Just static, Commander."

"Fire at the decoys. Loose!"

"God, man, no! You'll—" Volodya broke off, conscious that he was too late. Conscious too of what could happen should Dumarest be wrong and the ships, untouched by the flares if real, should fire back.

Dumarest calmed his fears. "They won't fire back."

"How can you be sure?"

"Just take my word for it."

A bald explanation but all he intended to give. The ships must have been sent by the Cyclan and the last thing the organization wanted was for him to be killed. Later, after they had won his secret, they would dispose of him but, until that time, he was too valuable to be risked.

"Three seconds," said the armiger. "Two. One—now!"

A flood of burning white radiance flowered in the void, dimming the light of the stars with the fury of a miniature man-made nova. The searing, expanding cloud touched the following vessels and destroyed them, while leaving the leading ships unharmed.

"Repeat the warning," snapped Dumarest. "And remind them the next torpedoes are for real."

Again a time of waiting and then, "They're gone!" The communication engineer yelled from his seat as he stared at the screens. "By, God, they've run!"

Vanishing into space as, wrapped in the blue cocoon of their Erhaft fields, the two vessels disappeared from sight.

Dumarest looked at where they had been, frowning, assessing their actions. To appear from two different directions at the same time accompanied by facsimile ships designed to frighten and intimidate. To ignore all attempts at contact and so, by silence, to enhance the terror of their menacing approach. Then, when their bluff had been called, simply to vanish and leave the guardians of Zabul staring wonderingly at where they had been.

Why?

Volodya had no doubts. "They've left," he said. "They came and tried to frighten us and when they found we had teeth decided to quit. A bluff, Earl, as you said."

A confidence Dumarest didn't share. To the technicians at the monitors he said, "Alter your scan. I want a thorough check of the surface." Then, as the screens changed to show the bizarre exterior of the artificial world and the tiny, antlike figures moving over it he said, "Not a bluff, Volodya, but a diversion. Now they're trying to break in."

The suit was tight, the flow of air a reassuring whisper in his ears, the surface of Zabul a firm solidity beneath hands and knees. Rising, he would be a clear target against the background of stars if anyone was watching from the shadows. To spring upward would be to break free of the gravity zone embracing Zabul. Drifting in space, even with guidance devices, he would be an even more helpless target.

All this he had tried to drive home to the members of the Corps before leaving the air-lock.

Some would remember, others, those trained for normal surface maintainance, would have no trouble, the rest, if they lived, would be lucky.

"In position, Commander." Medwin's voice vibrated from the speakers. "All units ready to go."

Their scrambled communication would be nothing more than a blur of static to outsiders. Dumarest checked his suit monitors, seeing air, temperature, humidity and ion level in the green. A precaution he'd tried to emphasize—too many new to suits had died for lack of automatic checking. Time became distorted when in an unaccustomed environment and changes in temperature and ion levels could alter normal perspective.

"Stand by." Then, to the scanning technicians, Dumarest said, "Any change in observed positions?"

"None." The voice sounded worried. "But they've started using thermal paste."

"Seal area in immediate vicinity. Inform if enemy changes positions." Then, to the Corps, "Right, we move in. Keep low and shoot first." And for God's sake hit the right targets, but he didn't mention that. The white flashes they wore would serve to identify them to each other if they took the time to look. "Ready? Go—and good luck!"

Dumarest felt the outer skin of Zabul scrape over his chest and thighs as, like a crab, he eased himself over the surface. The scanners had discovered the enemy busy at the foot of one of the towering pinnacles which dotted the curved and convoluted surface of Zabul. This surface had grown over the years as extensions had been made to the original plan, compartments added to the bulk of gutted vessels, space gained by rotund bulkheads. Now, illuminated by starlight, the fabrication resembled an ovoid, bristling with spines and blotched with warts. A dangerous world formed of declivities and slopes and enigmatic patches of shadow.

Something moved in one as Dumarest crawled near, a figure which paused, to rise and lift an arm. Dumarest rolled as heat followed the ruby guide beam of the laser.

"Hold it, you fool! What is your name?"

"What? I'm Varne. Kell Varne."

"Lower your gun! Do it!" Dumarest let anger sharpen his tone. "Now return to your entry port. See the officer in charge and place yourself under arrest. You're relieved of duty."

"But, sir, I—"

"No arguments! A man who will shoot a comrade isn't to be trusted with a gun. Now move before I burn you where you stand!"

An object lesson—the others would have heard and would now be more careful. The last he would give; the next man who threatened him would die no matter what uniform he wore. If he had allies in Command then Volodya could have friends in the Corps.

Dumarest moved on, reaching a narrow ridge, sliding over it to fall into a shallow declivity, reaching a level space where he paused to search the area ahead.

Starlight shimmered from reflective surfaces, revealing scars and rough patches, the spire of a scanning monitor, the tip of a distant tower. The horizon was near, too close for comfort, and the light made things deceptive. Was that a normal mound or the crouching figure of a man? Did that shadow come from a protuberance or from a watching guard?

And there would have to be guards—the brain which had planned the raid would not have neglected normal precautions. Men to work burning a hole through the surface, to reach the interior and then to use paralyzing gas to stun the inhabitants. Others to stand watch against surprise attack should the deception have failed, although that clever ruse had frozen the attention of Volodya and those in Command on the approaching vessels. Held it hard enough and long enough for a landing to be made on the surface of Zabul itself. But how had it been done?

A ship would have registered and been noticed despite the distraction. Sacs? The inflatable membranes would each have

held no more than three men at a squeeze—only one if he
was carrying equipment. Too many would have been needed
and maneuverability would have been a problem. What then?
Another facsimile?

Dumarest frowned as he stared ahead, then, to the scanning technicians, said, "Mark my position. Ahead and to my
right, too low for good vision, lies something long and ovoid.
Is it a natural part of Zabul?"

A moment while, high on a spire, the scanner of a relay
moved to study the area.

"No, Commander."

"Size?" Dumarest nodded as it was given. Not an exact
facsimile but something like one. A tough balloon fitted with
compressed air to give motion and direction, filled with men
and equipment and released far from Zabul on a flight path
which would bring it to a point within easy reach. Nonmetal-
lic, unmarked, a blur against the stars, it would have moved
too slowly to trigger the alarms. The approaching vessels had
made sure it would land without trouble.

But the diversion itself had warned Dumarest of the possibility.

He crawled sideways, reaching shadow and making his way
onward. From the speakers he heard a sudden rasp of breath,
a shout, a liquid gurgling followed by Medwin's voice.

"Kunel's dead! The bastards got him! Men! Let's get the
swine!"

"Hold it!" Dumarest rapped the command. "This is no
time for anger. Captain Medwin! Report!" He stressed the
title.

"Sorry, Commander." The speakers carried the sound of
ragged breathing. "I guess seeing him die got to me."

"Report, Captain!"

"We saw movement over to our right. That would be to
your left. Kunel must have got impatient and I saw him rise
and lope forward. He was a surface worker and knew how to
do it. Then there was a flash from ahead and I saw him rear
and go spinning upwards. Heard him too. Commander?"

"Stay low and keep calm. Kunel's dead, but that's war. He
grew careless and paid the price. A flash, you say?"

"Yes." Medwin was steadier now. "Just a point of light."

"A gun of some kind." Dumarest talked more to calm
young nerves than to give information. "A bullet projector.

They're hard to aim in conditions like this. Kunel was unlucky."

In more ways than one. The gun could have fired nothing more dangerous than an anesthetic dart but he had been caught off balance and sent to spin helplessly in space. Unconscious, with a perforated suit, the end was inevitable. Even if the puncture had been sealed with protective paste carried within the suit fabric he would still die of asphyxiation long before he could be rescued.

A matter Dumarest thought best not to mention. Instead he said, "Spread out and surround the enemy. Contain their field of operations. Hold your fire. If you shoot they'll fire back and we want no more casualties."

"As you say, Commander." Medwin was relieved at not having to make life-or-death decisions. "How are you going to handle the situation?"

"I'm going in," said Dumarest. "I'm giving them a chance to surrender."

Fire glowed as he moved forward over the curved area before him, a line of seething incandescence which died even as he watched to be reborn a little to one side. The thermal paste the technician had mentioned against which suited figures moved in blurred silhouettes. Dumarest counted six; too few for the capacity of the pod, and he guessed others must be busy elsewhere if not on guard.

Busy, but doing what?

He rolled so as to look upward at the slender spire tipped with the scanning eye and saw a figure climbing up toward it. A figure invisible to normal vision blocked as it was by the edge of the helmet. Once the eye had been blocked or destroyed the monitoring technicians would be partially blinded. If other eyes were taken out the invaders would have Zabul at their mercy.

A plan beaten by speed alone. Dumarest and the Corps he had set into position had acted too fast for the invaders to complete the operation.

Lifting the laser from its holster Dumarest aimed, fired, fired again, a third time. High above, the figure halted and began to work desperately at one leg. The first shot had missed, the second barely touching, the third burning flesh and perforating the suit. If the man was to live he had to seal the fabric and, with his leg injured, he could no longer reach the eye.

Static buzzed in his speakers as Dumarest moved on. Sharp bursts followed by others, signals from the enemy who, like the defenders, were using scrambled communication. Dumarest sprawled on the surface resting his helmet against the metal. Small sounds vibrated in his ears; noise transmitted by the solid medium. He heard a scrape, a cough, the sound of a metallic tapping. These clues guided him to where a man crouched behind a riveted protrusion. A guard who, too late, realized he was no longer alone.

"Move and you die!" Dumarest had touched his helmet to the other's, his voice carried by direct conduction. "How many of you are there?"

A burst of static came from his speakers, halting as he dug the muzzle of the laser deep into the suit and the flesh it enclosed.

"Just answer my question."

"Who the hell are you?"

"Someone short of patience. You want to talk or nurse broken elbows?"

"You're all mouth," sneered the man. "You haven't the guts."

"Try me." Dumarest waited then, as the man exploded into sudden action, moved back away from the swinging arm, lunging forward to lift the laser and send it smashing against the faceplate of the helmet. The blow starred the transparency but did not wholly break it. He heard the guard cry out as, again, their helmets touched. "Forget the elbows. Maybe you'd like to breathe vacuum instead."

"For God's sake, no!" The man lifted gloved hands to protect the damaged area. "I'm leaking air! Please, mister! You've done enough!"

"Then talk!"

"Yes. Just as soon as I've fixed this. Let me stick a seal over it and I'll tell you all you want to know."

"You'll tell me now. How many of you are there? Fifteen? Is that all?" The figure made sense. "Who is in command? Vellani? Contact him. Tell him I want to parley. Open channel. And I want him here. Warn him if he tries anything I'll burn the lot of you. Do it—then fix that helmet."

Vellani came within minutes, a bulky shape, huge in an ar-

mored suit. Starlight shone in reflected glimmers from mirrored plates protecting the joints and vital organs. The
faceplate was opaqued so that he loomed like a robot against
the stars. He came accompanied by three others who took up
positions around the area.

"You want to parley," he said without preamble. His voice
was deep, booming from the speakers. "All right, let's get on
with it. I'll accept unconditional surrender."

Dumarest said, "I was thinking of the reverse."

"A comedian. I've every one of your men marked and
mine are ready. A word and you'll lead nothing but cold
meat. In three minutes or less I'll be through the skin and
into Zabul. That's my hand—what's yours?"

"Strong enough to know you're bluffing."

"Maybe." Vellani stepped nearer. To the guard who had
stuck a transparent wafer over his faceplate he said, "Get
back with the others. Maybe later you'll wish this character
had finished the job."

"I did what I intended," said Dumarest. "You want to parley or waste time?"

"You don't sound right," mused Vellani. "You talk too
strong for a local. You a stranger?"

"Maybe."

"You could be the one I came for. In that case you've
saved me work and time." His hand lifted, the laser it held
aiming at Dumarest's knee. "You've got guts so I'm giving
you a choice. Be smart and cooperate and you'll stay in one
piece. Act dumb and I'll turn you into a basket case. Arms
off at the elbows, legs off at the knees. We'll seal the suit so
you won't lose too much air and the beam will cauterize the
wounds. I'll give you ten seconds to decide."

"How long have you commanded a combat team?"

"What?"

"Not long, I guess," said Dumarest. "Only a tyro would
give an opponent that much warning. Ten seconds! I could
kill you in the first two."

"And die yourself."

"Maybe, but what good would that do you?" Dumarest
turned to look at the others standing close. "Or you? Open
fire and you'll go down in a barrage. Do you think I'm stupid
enough to call a parley without taking precautions?"

One of the men shifted uneasily. He said, "He's got point, Jarl. And those locals could be trigger-happy."

"They're watching you now," said Dumarest. "Each of yo is sighted in their guns. You'd do damage, sure, but you' pay for it. Want a demonstration?"

From the speakers a voice said, "Give it to them, Com mander! Spill their guts! They killed Lars Kunel!"

"Silence! Who is that talking?" Dumarest frowned trying t remember the voice. "Kirek? Is that Captain Kirek?"

"That's right, Commander. If you're turning soft I'm no How about it, lads? Let's get the swine! Fire!"

"No, you fools! No!"

Dumarest lunged forward as he shouted, catching the bulky figure of Vellani at the waist, knocking him down as laser fire blazed around them. Beams hit and were reflected back from mirrored armor, searing the plates and protrusions of Zabul. Some hit more vulnerable targets.

A guard screamed as heat seared his faceplate and burned out his eyes. Another spun, blood spraying from his perforated suit. The third, faster, dropped, cursing, the weapon he held blasting a hail of missiles at suited figures who had risen to fire. Defenders who slumped or went twisting into space beneath the impact of hammering slugs.

"You bastard!" Vellani heaved to free himself. "You tricked us!"

"No," snapped Dumarest. "I played it straight and you know it. They've mutinied!"

Running wild beneath the surge of novel emotions, intoxicated with the power of their weapons, burning to avenge the death of a friend. A hysterical mob, firing, missing, dying as more experienced fighters fired in turn.

"The pod!" screamed Kirek. "Get the pod!"

Half the beams missed even so large a target. Half the rest did nothing but burn holes in the thin but rigid envelope. Of the rest some pitted the surface, a few came close to the invaders, one reached a heap of supplies waiting to be moved from the pod.

Explosives together with a mass of thermal paste, uncrated, primed, ready for use. The concentrated energy expanded into a ravening cloud as the laser triggered the reaction.

CHAPTER SIX

Dumarest stirred, tasting blood, conscious of the ache in his head, the dull agony of his left arm. He blinked, clearing his vision of residual glare, remembering the surge of transmitted vibration, the crashing impact of debris against his body and the back of his helmet. An impact which had slammed the faceplate hard against the surface. Listening to the gush of air, he felt the transparency, finding it uncracked. The air loss was due to another cause and he found it—a jagged rip beneath his left shoulder. A place almost impossible to reach with his one good arm.

Rolling he pressed the rip hard against the surface, blocking the flow while he stripped an adhesive wafer from the pack on his thigh. A lift and with an effort which sent blood roaring in his ears he managed to partially block the escape of air. Another wafer and the gushing roar eased a little. A third, spread on the surface over which he rolled, made the best repair he could manage.

Not good enough.

Too much air had gushed from his tanks as the regulator had tried to maintain internal pressure. Now, like a savage eye, the warning light was flashing from the gauge in his helmet.

"Attention all Corpsmen," he said into the radio. "Report!"

He heard nothing but the empty wash of static. Trying to contact the technicians produced the same result; the blow which had sent him to the verge of oblivion had damaged the radio. Rising, Dumarest looked around.

The pod had vanished, the equipment which had stood around it, the men working on the skin. The scintillating fury of the thermal paste was now nothing but a tenuous mass of dispersing vapor high in space where it had been blown by the rush of escaping air as it had burned through to the inner compartments.

Vellani was dead. He lay sprawled on the metal, his blank visor turned up toward the stars, face hidden beneath the opacity. But there was no need to see his face—the long, jagged shard of metal which had penetrated his suit despite the armor told its own story. The crude spear had smashed through heart and lungs to transfix the man as if he'd been an insect on a pin.

Had Dumarest been on the other side of the man it would be he now lying dead. Luck—for Vellani all of it bad.

Within his helmet the flashing red light steadied to erupt in a final warning glow. The last dregs of air had been fed from his tanks and Dumarest knew his life was now measured in minutes. He felt cold and could still hear a faint hiss, but this was not the comforting sound from the regulator but the lethal note of escaping air. To survive he had to reach a lock and get inside.

He turned, swaying, trying to orient himself. The lock he had used to reach the surface lay far back below the near horizon. Too far to travel in his present condition. There had to be another, closer, but where?

Dumarest sucked air into his lungs, held it while he forced himself to concentrate. His left arm hung limp at his side, broken or numbed, and the taste of blood in his mouth had grown stronger. Details he ignored as he scanned the area, aligning it with data culled from maps and charts. The nearest lock was over to his right below the curve of the surface. He must reach it or die.

Dumarest swung his right hand behind him, caught his left wrist and dragged the useless arm up and across his back. The soft hiss of escaping air faded as the constriction pressed against the rent. Carefully he stepped forward, stooping low, fighting the temptation to run.

To race was to lose—extra exertion would use up the remaining oxygen too fast. Yet to go too slowly was to invite destruction. If he tried to spring he could break free of the gravity zone to die helplessly in the void. Yet to crawl was to waste the seconds remaining.

Remembering Kunel, Dumarest began to lope.

It was a trick the surface worker had known and had used to run to his death. Now there was no enemy waiting with a gun but, equally, there was no body of experience on which to call. He had to lope, remaining low, not moving too fast yet using all the energy he could spare to throw himself over the surface toward the lock which spelled safety. Moving faster than a walk yet slower than a run, he fought to maintain his balance, to conserve his air, to remain alert as oxygen lack began to dull his mind and distort his judgment.

The lock rose before him, a cylindrical protuberance which swung against the backdrop of stars and blurred to take on the shape and form of a soaring pinnacle rising at an incredible distance over an endless plain. As illusion which yielded to another as Dumarest tripped to land heavily, pain stabbing from his arm, darkness edging his vision. Before him the cowled shape which the lock had become raised a hand to beckon, to turn into a crouching predator, to become a spined and wavering shape set in an eternity of sand.

Delirium. Hallucinations born in a tormented brain as he rose to forge on, feeling the pain from his bitten cheek, the taste of fresh blood mingling with that of old.

Again Dumarest fell, releasing the grip on his left wrist and feeling the sudden chill as air gushed from the opened vent, a signal which triggered the innate determination to survive which motivated his being. Rising, lungs burning, a red tide rising to tinge the universe with the hue of blood, he staggered forward into the embrace of the lock. A moment later he slammed his hand against the control, feeling the movement, falling forward as he was rotated into the inner compartment.

To fall, retching for air, as hands tore the helmet from his head.

"Commander!" Medwin stared at him, eyes wide, face shocked. "I thought you were dead!"

"Here!" A surface technician, more practical, thrust a mask beneath Dumarest's face. "Breathe deep, Commander. Deeply, now."

Life returned with the rush of pure oxygen and with it the

pain. His arm, the bitten cheek, the throbbing in his head, the raw agony of his lungs. Dumarest coughed, spat blood, swallowed more.

The technician said, "You're going down to medical, Commander. You've sucked vacuum and those lungs need treatment."

"Later." Dumarest looked at Medwin. "What are you doing here, Captain? Get some men and go out searching. Your comrades could need you."

"They're dead, Commander. All dead."

"You can't be sure of that." Dumarest sucked more oxygen into his lungs, the gas seeming to be acid boiling within his chest. Pain sharpened his tone. "I wasn't. Others could be lying out there this minute. Hurt. Waiting for help. Get out there, damn you! Get out and look!"

"Steady, Commander." The technician adjusted the flow of oxygen. "Just take things easy."

"Use the radio," snapped Dumarest. "Men could have been thrown into the void when the fireball was blasted from the surface. Count heads. I want every man accounted for. Bring them all inside. Understand? All of them."

Medwin said, dubiously, "The enemy too?"

"All of them!"

"Better do it," said the technician. Then, to Dumarest, "All right, Commander. Let's get you down to the infirmary."

Sneh Thorne finished checking the dressing and, straightening, said, "You were lucky, Earl. A damned sight luckier than most."

"Tell me."

"Those young fools didn't stand a chance. They went out there and most of them stayed. A few made it back and some managed to stay unhurt. The rest—" He broke off, his gesture expressive. "Soldiers," he added bitterly. "The glory of war."

"There is no glory in war," said Dumarest. "There's only death and pain and destruction. But those men weren't soldiers. They weren't fools either. They had the guts to go out and do what had to be done to protect your nice, snug little world. Did Alva Kirek make it back?"

"No. Not alive if that's what you mean. Did you have a special interest in him?"

Alive he would have been arrested, charged, tried and executed for having incited the mutiny which had created such havoc. Dead he was no longer a problem Dumarest had to deal with.

Rearing upright in the bed he threw his legs over the edge and looked at his arm. The bicep was bulky with a transparent dressing.

"The bone was broken," explained Thorne. "I've fixed it and you've been under slow time—three weeks subjective—so if you feel hungry you know why. You can use the arm if you want to, but it would be best to use a sling for a while." He gestured to where it lay together with Dumarest's clothing. "You also had concussion and vacuum-burned lungs. That pure oxygen must have burned like hell. Well, it's all fixed now and you can leave when you want." He added bitterly, "Leave to spread your infection."

"Meaning?"

"I spoke of it before, remember? You're like a virus. What you touch turns bad. You encourage violence. Those young men who died out there. The ones who came back more dead than alive. If you hadn't been here would it have happened?"

Dumarest said softly, "If you had never been born could you ever die?"

"What has that to do with it?"

"Things are what they are. Life isn't gentle. Did you think it was?"

"No," admitted Thorne. "And I know what you're getting at. Althea told me and, as a medical man, I must agree. The process of life is a continual act of violence, but does that mean man has to kill man?"

"If it is in order to defend himself—yes."

"But—"

"You blame me for those who died," said Dumarest. "You should blame yourselves. They were raw, untrained, totally unused to combat. I did what I could but it wasn't enough. Faced with cold reality they lost their heads and paid the penalty. That's what life is all about. The survival of the fittest. You win or you lose. You live or you die."

"Kill or be killed," snapped Thorne. "Is that it?"

"An organism must protect itself."

"Or fall prey to another." Thorne shook his head. "Man, you don't belong here. You preach the law of the jungle."

The jungle the race had never left. Which accompanied every man and woman all the days of their lives no matter where they lived or how. The basic rule of survival, ignored, spelled extinction.

Dumarest rose and dressed and lingered for a moment before stepping from the room. Outside Althea was waiting, her eyes widening as she saw the sling supporting his left arm.

"It's nothing." He smiled so as to relieve her anxiety. "Just a little soreness. What's been happening?"

"Too much." Her face was drawn, fatigue creasing the soft skin around her eyes. "The committee has been in session for hours and there have been urgent matters to attend to. Volodya has taken over, a virtual dictator—on the grounds of necessity, he claimed. Brandt was with him as were Lijert and Stanton. Prideaux objected but was beaten at the vote when Towitsch sided with Volodya. So there it is." The gesture of her hands was one of defeat. "It's been a long day, Earl."

Hours which for him had been weeks, but he had been resting drugged and unconscious, fed by artificial means while she had had to face the opposition alone.

Dumarest said, "What of the Corps?"

"I don't know."

"The men who went outside with me? What is the position?" Thorne could have lied. "I know Medwin is alive but who else?"

She said, "You had five teams each of a dozen men and each with its own captain. Of the five Medwin and Quiley are still alive though Quiley was hurt. Of the men eighteen returned alive and a dozen of them are injured. Half will be lucky to make it."

Those losses had to have an adverse effect on morale. No wonder Thorne had been so bitter. Dumarest said, "What of the others?"

"The enemy? None were found alive."

Or if alive had not lived long. That was a possibility but Dumarest discounted it; the Terridae were too gentle for ruthless murder. "Their bodies?"

They were down near the reclamation plant, stretched in a ragged line, stripped of their suits and looking like broken and discarded dolls. A half-dozen of them, more than Dumarest had expected. Hard-faced men bearing a common stamp. Mercenaries, trading in war, selling their skills and obedience to any willing to pay. Vellani lay to the far end, his hair cropped to form a dark cap over a peaked skull. His face was broad, the mouth cruel, a scar running over one cheek. A proud man who wore his name blazoned on the black and gold of his uniform. A wolf and the leader of wolves.

"From Sorkendo," said Althea when Dumarest glanced at her. "We searched them and found papers from that world. Some bills, a program to a local spectacle, some stamped photographs of women."

"Vellani?"

"Nothing. His pockets were empty aside from a medical pack containing a variety of drugs and some packs of narcotic gum." She added, "He carried a laser in a sleeve holster and wore heavy rings."

The mark of a professional. Dumarest said, "He was the leader and the others must have been recently hired for the job. From Sorkendo?"

"According to their papers. It's a world lying toward the Zaragoza Cluster. I could find out how far if you want."

But that was academic. The men had come and been defeated; now other problems remained. Had they comrades in space? How long would they wait? Who had hired them and why?

The last question at least he could answer. Who but the Cyclan wanted to hunt him down?

Althea said, "One other thing, Earl. Those ships we saw which vanished—they've come back. Volodya has invited one to land."

It hung in space inching gently toward the port, smooth, sleek, obviously well-maintained. A free-trader which had been adapted and Dumarest could guess why. At his side as he watched it in the screen Volodya said, "The *Moira* commanded by Captain Pendance. I thought it best to permit him to land and discuss the situation."

"You must have had a long talk."

"Long enough."

"For what? To be conned? Where is the other ship? Waiting out there ready to blast Zabul to scrap if the *Moira* is threatened?"

"There is no other ship," said Volodya. "It's gone. We deal with Captain Pendance alone."

An illusion and he was a fool if he believed it, but Dumarest sensed that Volodya was acting with calculated intent. Sensed too the augmented aura of power he wore, which was betrayed in his stance, the tilt of his head, the tone of his voice—the trappings of arrogance born of the knowledge of total command.

Volodya had gained that command while Dumarest had been under sedation and, with a gambler's instinct, Dumarest knew he held a losing hand.

"I think we should greet them," said Volodya as the ship reached the lock. "It would be a courteous gesture and I do not want them in Command. Major!" He looked expressionlessly at Dumarest as Medwin entered and snapped to attention. "Is the lock area sealed?"

"Yes, sir."

"Then conduct us to meet our visitors."

An illustration of power neatly done. Dumarest looked at the young man now wearing the uniform of Volodya's guards.

"So you're a major now. Congratulations on the promotion."

Medwin stared past him, his face twitching.

"Don't feel bad about it." Dumarest adjusted the sling on his left arm. "We all have to look after ourselves and a smart man knows when it's time to change sides. Keep going as you are and, soon, you may even reach the top." He added, looking at Volodya, "That's when your troubles really begin."

"The door," snapped Volodya. "Hurry, Major—our visitors will be waiting."

They stood within the lock area, five of them, four wearing tough, practical clothing, the other dressed in ornate finery. He stepped forward as Volodya approached, lifting a hand heavy with rings, gems catching and reflecting the light in dancing shimmers as, gesturing, he smiled.

"This is a pleasure, sir. Captain Pendance at your service. And this is the gentleman we spoke of? Again my pleasure. I am certain we can all be friends."

Dumarest said, "What do you want?"

"Want?" Pendance glanced at Volodya then back at

Dumarest. "Why, just to talk a little. To clear up certain misunderstandings To share a rare and costly wine. Bisdon! The wine for our hosts. Use the special glasses. Made of Surrentian crystal," he explained as one of his men produced a box and took out a bottle. "It touches the lips like a passionate kiss. I bore you?"

"No wine," said Dumarest. "Not for me." Then, speaking to Medwin and the other guards rather than the visitors, he said, "I assume you've come to discuss the matter of compensation and to make apologies for your wanton and unprovoked attack on this world and its people. How many died, Volodya? I'm sure you have the figure. Something like six dozen, wasn't it? And another score badly injured. Call it a hundred casualties. How much a head do you offer, Captain Pendance?"

The figure was exaggerated but the captain couldn't argue and for Volodya to protest would make him appear to be diminishing the importance of the losses.

Pendance said, "Offer? I fail to understand."

"Then start with an apology. At least pretend to regret your men attacked Zabul."

"You assume too much!" For a moment Pendance's facade dropped to reveal a little of the true man beneath. Not a decorated fop but someone who was cruel and vicious and a stranger to mercy. Then he was smiling again and the moment had passed. "I understand your attitude but, believe me, I am innocent. It was the other ship which launched the attack. It was their men you killed—they are dead, are they not? A pity. Under interrogation they would have cleared me of supicion." Then, to Volodya, "But to get back to the matter at hand, sir. Shall we drink a little wine to seal our bargain?"

"No wine." Volodya looked at Dumarest. "I've no choice," he said. "Surely you can see that?"

"A man always has a choice."

"Not in this case. Captain?"

"The weakness of a man lies in love," said Pendance. He accepted a glass from his aide and lifted it to show the golden fluid it contained. The wine was held in the glass shaped like an upturned hand, which seemed to quiver as if with a life of its own. "Beautiful, is it not? The work of

genius and the wine matches the glass. If you knew me better
you would realize how high is my regard for you that I offered to share it. To your health, sir." Looking at Volodya he
took a sip. Then, to Dumarest, "To your health."

"You spoke of love."

"Ah, yes, so I did." Pendance touched a scrap of fabric to
his lips. "The love of things, Earl. The love of a woman. But,
above all, the love of authority. For such a love a man will
forget his pride. He will kill, steal, betray a friend. How,
much easier, then, it would be for him to rid himself of a
rival."

"Me?"

"You are a man of discernment. But can you blame him?
You, the victor of the recent unpleasantness, must surely pose
a threat. The young love courage and acts of heroism performed under staggering difficulties. We know better but we
have had time in which to learn. Time, the enemy of us all."
He lifted his free hand as, again, he sipped at his wine. A
gesture which seemed to command silence as it drew attention. "A rare moment," he said as he lowered the glass.
"Good things should be savored to the full. Wine, a meal, a
woman." He laughed with a strange cacophony. "Even a
fight. At times I think combat alone can teach what lies
within a man. The scent of blood, the touch of pain, the sight
of death—and the weaklings run."

They change sides as Medwin had done, persuaded by Volodya's arguments, Thorne's hatred of violence and, even, his
own fears. The reality of war had changed more than one
strutting braggart into a wincing coward.

How many of the Corps had followed his example?

Dumarest turned, fumbling with his sling but keeping his
free hand in full view. The guards ringing the area contained
faces he recognized but to appeal to them would be a waste
of time. They would accept Volodya's authority. Obey his orders. Carry out his commands. Later, as he must have told
them, he would lead them to the Event.

Later—a thousand years, perhaps. He would be in no
hurry.

"The wine," said Pendance. "I really must insist you take
some wine. Bisdon! Give him a glass—and make sure he
holds it in his left hand."

Dumarest waited until the man came close then drew back the sling to show his empty fingers. They rested lax in the fabric and the man had to push the glass between them.

"That's better." Pendance smiled his satisfaction. "Who knows what a hidden hand could hold? I have no wish to harm you, Earl, but—"

"I know. Try anything and you'll burn my legs off at the knees. My arms at the elbows. I've heard it all before."

"Yet managed to remain intact. You're a most unusual person and we must talk at length later when on our way."

"To where?"

"Does it matter? Let us just say that certain mutual acquaintances are eager for your company and are willing to pay highly for the privilege."

"And if I offered more?"

Regretfully Pendance shook his head. "You would only waste time. There are certain ethical considerations, you understand. And our mutual friends are not to be trifled with. I suggest you drink your wine and put an end to what could become an awkward situation. No guest should outstay his welcome and I'm sure your host would be reluctant to use force."

A reluctance he would overcome. Dumarest glanced to where Volodya now stood, flanked by his guards. Men he recognized who had no cause to be gentle. They would use clubs or gas and no matter how hard he fought the end would be the same.

"No," said Pendance softly. "Don't try it. You are a hawk among pigeons but, my friend, even the strongest and most courageous of beasts can be pulled down by a pack of snapping curs. You have done what you could for these people and in return they have sold you out. Why give them the satisfaction of adding injury to insult?" Without moving his eyes he snapped, "Bisdon! Pack up the wine. Be careful when you collect the glass from our new companion."

The wine he hadn't tasted. Dumarest held it out as the man came close, using his right hand to lift the arm in the sling. A natural gesture followed by another as he felt it plucked from his fingers. A step followed by a stumble which threw him against the man and knocked him off-balance.

"The glass!" Pendance shouted the warning. "Be careful, you fool!"

A moment when his attention was distracted. When every eye was on Bisdon and his frantic attempts to save the crystal from ruin.

Dumarest thrust his right hand into the sling, found the ampule of slow time he had hidden there and thrust the needle into his arm.

CHAPTER SEVEN

The lights flickered and the room became full of statues. Dumarest slowly withdrew the ampule from his arm and threw it to one side where it burst like a miniature bomb against a wall. Before him Bisdon seemed to hang suspended in mid-air, eyes wide, mouth gaping, one hand clutching the precious glass. Beyond him Pendance had one foot lifted, his body leaning forward, frozen in mid-stride.

Volodya, the guards, the rest of Pendance's crew—all were frozen in various attitudes.

An illusion; they hadn't changed but Dumarest's metabolism had speeded to forty times normal. He could see and move and act at the accelerated speed but there were dangers. He could move forty times as fast but he wasn't forty times as strong. If he punched a man he would shatter bone and pulp flesh—his own as well as the victim's. A knock was a blow which could break bones in his hands and leave bruised flesh. To move at all was to create a hampering wind and to shift objects was to fight against their increased inertia which showed itself as a massive gain in weight.

But there had been no other way to escape from the jaws of the trap Volodya had sprung.

Dumarest stepped toward the door leading to Command and halted as he saw it was closed and blocked by a heavyset guard. To shift both would take too much time and too much energy. Turning he studied the compartment. The lock itself was unguarded and various items of equipment stood or were racked against the walls. In the screen the ship hung connected to the outer door by a flexible communication tube.

Wind droned past his ears as Dumarest stepped toward equipment standing ready for use when vessels had to be loaded or compartments freed of their cargo. Wrecking bars, snips, extinguishers which could spout a mass of fire-dampening foam. Suits hung on a rack together with sacs for personal transportation through space for short distances. Next to a compressor stood ranked tanks of air.

Dumarest reached down and gripped one, straining as he lifted, remembering to take his time and not to grip too hard. Slowly it rose and he gripped it in both hands, ignoring the ache from the newly healed bone in his left arm. With it poised above his head he launched it with all his strength at a point above and to one side of the lock. As it left his hands he turned and picked up a slender bar.

It lifted more easily and he thrust it at the bulk of an alarm, shattering the case and shorting inner connections. Havoc repeated in three other places before he threw the bar like a spear at the deep indentation left by the tank of air.

As he saw it penetrate he moved quickly into the lock.

It rotated with dragging slowness finally to give access to the connecting tube. Three steps and he was at the ship. The lock was open and he stepped inside to pause for a moment as he assessed the situation.

A gamble, but if he had guessed right the vessel must be near-deserted. Vellani and his men must have come from the *Moira* and they, together with Pendance and his men, would almost have emptied the ship. He based this calculation on the reluctance of mercenaries and free-traders to split profits more than they had to; the pod and decoys must have taken a lot of space.

Dumarest swayed as the outer port swung closed. He was burning fuel at an enormous rate and had only recently used slow time before. His body tissue, wasted then, was being used now to his detriment. Unless he neutralized the drug and ate, he could, literally, starve to death or collapse from dehydration.

Within the ship he paused then headed for the engine room where the engineer was usually to be found. He was sitting at his console, head slumped on his arms, apparently asleep. The hold was empty as were the cabins and salon. No handler, then, and no steward or they had accompanied Pendance. But surely he must have left more than one man to guard the vessel?

He was in the control room, a stylishly dressed man of late middle age who sat in the pilot's chair with one hand supporting his chin while his eyes remained fastened on a screen. It pictured Zabul and the lock to which the ship was connected and, already, Dumarest could see the expanding plume of escaping air from the hole he had made.

This was a minor emergency which could easily be handled by the technicians, but he had aggravated it by smashing the alarms and so helped to create a greater degree of confusion.

A device to gain time; by the time things had settled he hoped to be well away.

Lights flickered on the control panels, moving even to his accelerated sense of vision, and he guessed the *Moira* was monitoring the environment for a wide area around. Each drifting mote of debris or movement of the structure would be sensed, checked, assessed and registered.

Leaning forward Dumarest checked the controls. A switch would break the connection with the tube in case of emergency and he threw it, seeing the flexible connection draw back to Zabul as the ship began gently to drift away impelled by the gust of expelled air. The gap widened but too slowly for his liking and Dumarest frowned as he studied the controls. They were unfamiliar, more complex than those of normal free-traders, proof as to his earlier suspicions.

Then, as he straightened, something ground into the base of his neck.

"Don't move your hands," said a voice. "Just hold them from your sides. Good. Now lift them and lock fingers on the top of your head. That's right. Now back out and keep backing until you're in the salon." A sigh as he obeyed. "Now you can turn."

He faced a woman.

She was tall and lithe with a copper-hued skin and long hair black as night which hung in thick braids over her shoulders and the high promontories of her breasts. A creature of the wild with high cheekbones and flared nostrils and eyes of liquid ebon deep-set beneath thick brows. Her mouth was full, the lower lip pouting with betraying sensuosity, the chin rounded and with a dimpled cleft. Facts he noted as he assessed the broad shoulders and narrow waist, the rounded hips and long, swelling curves of her thighs and calves.

Details lost in the forceful blaze of her personality as she stood, staring at him, the peculiar gun she carried pointed at his face.

"You're fast," she said. "So am I with this dope but in case you think you've an edge you'd better think again. I'm using a laser, wide-spread beam like a fan. No trigger that takes time to operate but an induction button instead. Move and I'll touch it and unless you can jump ten feet to one side you'll be burned. Ten feet at a speed as fast as light," she added. "Can you do it?"

"No."

"Just that? Nothing else?"

Dumarest said dryly, "I'm in no position to argue. Can I lower my hands?" He did so as she nodded. "How did I miss you?"

"I should be asking the questions."

"And why the slow time?"

"A precaution," she said. "I was checking and noticed signals which shouldn't have been so I took a shot of slow time just in case. When you searched I just moved from one cabin to another while out of your sight. You're Dumarest, right?"

"Earl Dumarest, yes. And you?"

"Ysanne."

"Ysanne who?"

"Just that. Ysanne. Where I come from we only use one name. Why were you stealing the *Moira*?"

He said bluntly, "In order to save my life. Can you think of a better reason?"

"If I were in your position, probably not," she agreed. "But I haven't your problem and don't want to share it." She frowned as he swayed. "Don't try it if you're thinking of jumping me. And don't think I won't use this if I have to." She gestured with the gun. "I had it specially made to take care of characters who think a woman's easy prey." Her tone changed a little. "Are you ill?"

"Weak. I've been in slow time too long. Can we get away from here so I can neutralize?"

For a moment she stared at him then, throwing back her head, filled the salon with genuine laughter.

"Man, you're the most! What makes you think I'd abandon Pendance and the others? And for what?"

"Money," said Dumarest. "A lot of money. And a ship. And, maybe, just for the hell of it."

A gamble but now luck was with him and he relaxed a little as, again, her laughter pealed through the salon. A woman but more than that. An adventuress, a kindred soul—he had sensed it as an animal could sense its mate over miles of frozen terrain. Then, as he saw her face change, he realized it had been a two-way exchange.

"Here!" She handed him a hypogun. "Neutralize while I put the *Moira* into a course away from Zabul."

"Heading toward the other ship," Dumarest added, as she stared at him. "And radio to let them know you have me safe. Arrange a rendezvous for the exchange."

"I thought you wanted to escape."

"That's the idea."

He lifted the hypogun as she left the salon and aimed it at his throat before pulling the trigger. Air blasted a charge of drugs into his bloodstream and he felt a momentary vertigo as his metabolism slowed back to normal. He was on his third cup of basic when Ysanne returned. He handed her one as she, suddenly, stood before him.

"Here! You must be hungry."

"I can go without food for a week at a time."

"So can anyone if they have to." Dumarest swallowed more of the liquid. It was loaded with protein, sickly with glucose, tart with added vitamins. A cup provided a spaceman with enough energy for a day. "Who is that in the control room?"

"Maynard. The second in command. He won't bother us." Ysanne lifted the hypogun in explanation. "I gave him a shot to put him out so we can talk. And I told Craig to stay where he is."

"The engineer?"

"That's right. Did you see his face?"

"No."

"It's burned," she said. "Pendance's work. A dose of acid when the generator went on the blink. If he weren't so good he'd be dead by now. Persuade me and he'll ride along."

"Persuade?"

"The money. The adventure. You think I'm doing this just

because I like your face? You're valuable property, I know that, but just how damned valuable? And why? Did I tell you I was curious?"

More than curious and with a feline grace which emphasized the contours of her face, the dark glitter of her eyes. They were ebon pools which widened as he talked then narrowed with sudden speculation, calmed as she made her evaluation.

"You're mad," she said. "But it's the kind of craziness I go for. To hunt down a legend! Well, there are worse things."

"Like slaving?"

"That depends on which side you're on. Pendance made it pay."

"So you went along with it?"

"Sure. Why not? There are worse things."

"Not if you've ever worn a collar." Dumarest changed the subject, like the cat she seemed she was amoral. For her the concepts of good and evil did not exist. A fact he recognized but one overlaid by the necessity to win her cooperation. "Work," he said. "Ship after ship, world after world. After a dozen they all seem the same. I'm giving you a chance to break free."

"To find Earth," she said. "Crazy, but I like the idea. I told you that. Just put up the money and I'm with you." She sobered as he remained silent. "You've got the money? No? Then how the hell do you expect to get where you want to go?

"In the *Moira*."

"And how do you expect to pay for fuel? Supplies? A crew?"

Dumarest said, "I'm valuable, you know that, and you know who is willing to pay. So I'm your insurance. Trust me a little and, if I don't deliver, then you collect from those who paid Pendance to get me." He added casually, "How far is the other ship?"

"Not far."

"You know who is in it?"

"A cyber. I heard him on the radio." She frowned as she considered his suggestion but he had narrowed her field of choice. To return now to Pendance would be to invite acid in the face. To sell Dumarest would be to lose the chance of an intriguing adventure. To do nothing would be to go against her restless nature. "You bastard," she said. "You cunning bastard. You tricked Pendance and stole his ship and now you want to use it for free. Well, why not?"

"A crew. We've got an engineer if you can talk Craig into it as you promised. Maynard might act as our captain but what about a navigator?"

"You've got one. Me. The finest in space." She smiled at his expression. "I mean that—or haven't you ever met a woman who's good at anything outside of a bed?"

"Words aren't deeds. How soon do we reach that other ship?"

"Why? What's the interest? We're not going to hit it."

"Wrong. That's just what I want to do." Dumarest forced himself to be patient as he explained. To emphasize the danger was to sow the seeds of potential panic, to minimize it would breed carelessness. "Pendance is back in Zabul. I tried to gain time so as to get clear but he'll want to radio the other ship. You got in first so they may suspect a trap or decide to play both sides. We are closest so it will be logical for them to keep the rendezvous and jump us as soon as they get the chance. We have to prevent them from doing that."

"Or?" She answered her own question. "They'll pick up Pendance and his men and come after us. With a faster ship and a full crew they'll trail and catch us for sure. When they do—" She broke off, thinking of the engineer and his ruined face. "What do you want to do, Earl?"

Smash the other ship from space, destroy the poison it contained, wipe the threat from the universe as he would rid his body of a venomous insect. Instead he had to compromise. To make do with what he had.

She nodded when he explained. "We'll need Maynard. I'll talk him into it while you take care of Craig. He'll help you get things ready if you handle him right. But hurry, man, we've got less than an hour!"

Craig was thick-set, stocky, a man who carried his brains in his hands and the marks of Pendance's anger on his face. The skin was blotched, oozing with sores, tissue stretched like thin red paper over the bone, a clownlike mask from which blue eyes gleamed beneath shaggy brows. His hair was rust-colored, short, bristling in angry spikes.

Looking around the hold he said, "That's about the best we can do, Earl. To gather more will take time we haven't got."

"You've done well, Jed."

"Maybe." Craig lifted a hand as if to rub his chin then, remembering, lowered it to his side. A thwarted gesture he felt he should explain. "It's the sores. Touching them makes it worse."

"They can be treated. The rest too."

"Sure." Craig looked at his hands. They were broad, scarred, the tips of his fingers spatulate. "I guess you wonder how I let them get away with it. Pendance, I mean and the acid. Did Ysanne tell you about it?"

"Briefly. Not the details."

"He was in a rage and when he's in that state he'll kill as soon as breathe. The generator—well, never mind that now. I'd done my best but it wasn't good enough and he threw the acid. I'd been cleaning a component and it was standing on the bench. Maybe he didn't know what was in the beaker."

"Maybe."

"Or maybe I'm just trying to fool myself. Is that what you think?"

"It's none of my business," said Dumarest. "We all do odd things at times—act the fool, the idiot, the amateur."

"The coward?"

"That too at times if there's no other choice. Or to seem to act that way to those with no right to judge. At times to be brave is to be dead. A smart man recognizes the situation, waits his chance then, when it comes, takes his revenge."

"Like now." Craig straightened his shoulders, his pride restored. "Maybe he'll remember what he did after we're through."

The captain and the cyber now waited in the ship ahead. Dumarest wondered if even now he was assessing the situation, extrapolating the probabilities and arriving at a prediction of what could happen. He hoped not; the chances were small enough without a trained and calculating mind making them less.

He looked at what had been gathered in the hold; the piles of scrap, the supplies left by the mercenaries, old tools, sections of metal cut and fashioned into jagged scraps. Items small enough to be handled and heavy enough to contain a respectable mass.

From a speaker Ysanne said, "We're getting close, Earl. You'd better get ready."

"Is everything under control?"

"Of course." Her voice held amusement and something else; an emotion close to euphoria, the intoxication of the senses now sharpened to a fine pitch. One he recognized. "Don't worry about this end, just concentrate on your own. I'll give you the timing."

To Craig Dumarest said, "We'll suit up now and loosen the hatches. Make certain your line is secure."

They both checked and then there was nothing to do but wait. Dumarest could hear the sound of the engineer's breathing in his speakers, a soft susurration which could have been static or the rustle of a woman's clothing. Ysanne? She was with Maynard and he wondered how she had gained the man's cooperation. With lies, he guessed, a tale acceptable to a drugged mind. With smiles and promises and the warm allure of her body. Such a woman would stop at nothing to get her own way.

"We're in contact," she said from the radio. "They want to talk to Pendance."

"Tell them we left him back in Zabul."

"Why?"

"We want to make a special deal. Use your imagination but don't lie unless you have to."

Lies would warn without need and the cyber would be wary as it was. He must know where Pendance was but would also be aware of the greed which drove men into strange paths.

"I don't think they're buying it, Earl."

"Be open. We'll come to a halt and they can check. What can they lose?" He added, "Don't be too polite. You have what they want and let them know it. How much longer?"

"Minutes now. Stand by."

"Stand by the hatches, Jed." Dumarest took up his position, conscious of the prickling of his back, the tension which always warned of danger. Automatically he checked his line, the instruments within his helmet, the position of the assembled debris. The enemy lay outside. "Ysanne?"

"Seconds now before we drop the field." A pause, then, "On three, Earl. One! Two! Three! Now!"

The hatches swung open beneath the engineer's hands,

space filling the frame of the structure, the bulk of the other
ship almost dead center. Good aiming and even better navigation but there was no time to assess the skills of the pilot
and the girl.

"Now!" snapped Dumarest. "Now!"

He threw his weight against a heap of scraps and thrust
them into the void. More followed, sacks which broke to spill
their contents, containers tipped to spread their loads, all the
items collected, the rubbish and pieces and unessential furnishings of the hold and workroom. The mass spread into
space, carrying with it the momentum of the ship—which
was aimed at the vessel lying dead ahead.

Surprise was their only asset. Given time the ship would
move, run from the hail, find safety in its Erhaft field, but
Dumarest had given them no time. The ship they were ex-
pecting had arrived, killed its field to coast to the rendezvous.
The mass of debris was masked by its bulk, the scanners of
the other vessel unable to isolate the fragments.

"Up!" snapped Dumarest. "Up and away!"

The picture framed in the open hatch changed as he was
obeyed. Stars replacing the ship, the widening hail heading
toward it. A rain which hit the vessel, tearing into the hull,
perforating it, ruining the scanners and creating internal
chaos.

"We did it!" yelled Craig. "By God, we did it!" He
laughed as he closed the hatches, slipping, saved from falling
into space by the line at his waist. Dumarest crossed to it and
hauled the man to safety before sealing the hatches.
"Ysanne!"

"I know, Jed." Her voice was as light as the engineer's. "A
crazy scheme but it worked. That ship won't move in a
hurry. Where to now?"

"Anywhere." Dumarest cracked his suit as the external
pressure reached normal. "Just get moving. We can change
course later."

Change it again and yet again in a random pattern to
throw off pursuit. He would decide that later but, for now, the
euphoria was enough, and was shared by Ysanne, as he could
see when she came to join him in the salon.

"Earl!" She stood close before him. "By, God—Earl!"

She was like a gambler lost in the intoxication of success,
exaggerated by the tensions which had preceded it, now

blazing from every atom of her being. This was a feeling he knew and had seen too often—the reward of all who deliberately risked their lives and so played with the highest stake of all.

He felt her nearness, the warm exudations of her body, and felt himself respond to her need. The light caught the heavy braids of her hair, creating a small aura of haze touched with color. The oil which gave it added sheen carried a heavy, pungent scent.

"You bitch! You dirty, lying bitch!"

Maynard had entered the salon and now stood to one side of the door. His face was tense, his eyes rimmed with red, angry, bloodshot. The collar of his tunic was open and Dumarest could see the thick veins pulsing in his neck beneath the mottled skin. He had arisen from a drugged acquiescence to vent a killing rage.

"Don't move!" he said. "Just don't either of you move!"

The gun he carried was the one Ysanne had used and Dumarest knew the fan would cover the entire area of the salon where they stood. A device used by slavers to control their victims, burning with savage intensity even if it did not kill.

Dumarest said, "What's the matter? Why the gun?"

"Stay out of this. Move over to one side. Move, damn you!" The jerk of the gun emphasized the command. "Get away from her!"

"Do it, Earl." Then, as he obeyed, she said, "I had to do it, Evan. It was for the best."

"Your best or mine?" His hand shook with renewed anger. "Using me. Lying. Promising—and for what? You know who that ship carried? You know what the Cyclan do to those who work against them? We had a fortune in our hand and you threw it away. I ought to burn your eyes out."

"You wouldn't like me if you did." Her eyes were direct, her tone loaded with hidden meaning. "You're upset and you've a right to be annoyed, but if you'll just let me explain. There wasn't time before. Now, if you'd just listen we can straighten all this out." She stepped toward him, one hand extended. "Give me the gun and let's forget this nonsense."

Dumarest watched, admiring her calm, yet aware of the tension Maynard was under. Jealousy compounded with fear, the two creating a suicidal rage. Death would offer him an escape from his problems and, killing her, would insure his possession. Soon now he would act—if she took a few steps closer he would explode or collapse. Kill or cry.

Only then would he have a chance.

As Ysanne moved closer, talking as if to a child, Dumarest studied the man, the gun he held. It was a fan-beam, which meant the energy would be dispersed. The induction button gave no delay but his finger still had to touch it. A tiny movement compared to that he would have to take but if the woman was out of the field of fire it would ease the problem.

He said, "Drop, girl! Drop!"

"What?" Maynard turned toward him. "What's that you say?"

Ysanne tried to take advantage of this distraction. Her long legs moved, her hand reaching out for the gun, missing as Maynard jerked it back, lifting his free hand to send it slashing across her face. The blow sent her staggering back, to trip, to fall sprawling on the floor.

"You bastard! You—no, Earl! Earl!"

He had stooped, right knee lifting, hand rising weighted with his knife. Steel flashed as the knife spun across the salon when Maynard fired. One shot which died as metal touched his throat, drove deep into skin and fat and muscle, cutting the great arteries and the flow of blood to the brain.

"Earl!" Ysanne rose, ignoring the blood, the dead man on the floor. "He shot you!"

The heat had missed his face, his hands, burning instead a narrow swath across his tunic, searing the plastic and revealing the metal mesh buried within the material. This protection had absorbed the energy and saved him from injury.

"No harm," she said. "Thank God for that." Then, looking at the dead man, she added, "But what do we do now for a captain?"

CHAPTER EIGHT

Every ship carried ghosts and a slaver more than most; whispers, sighs, cries of pain and grief, the slurry of restless movement. Vibrations caught and transmitted through the structure to fade and die in murmuring susurrations. But, in the *Moira*, the ghosts Dumarest heard were things of silence.

The ship was too quiet. In the engine room Jed Craig tended the humming generators and in the control room watchful mechanisms studied the space through which they drove but here, in the cabin, he heard nothing but the small sounds created by the woman at his side.

She moved as he glanced at her, one hand lifting to touch his arm, her lips smiling as her fingers met his flesh. She was newly awake as he could tell from the altered tempo of her breathing yet remembered a recent passion which, slaked, had left them satiated.

A single point of light illuminated the cabin with a soft, pink glow and he remembered another room, another woman revealed in a similar illumination.

As if reading his mind Ysanne said, "Regrets, Earl?"

"No."

"Memories, then? Of someone you left behind in Zabul?" Her hand moved over his naked torso. "Someone who loved you?"

A question he left unanswered even as he wondered why he found it so hard to remember Althea's face. Copper hair and emerald eyes—familiar coloration, but she had lacked

the raw energy which filled Ysanne. The same burning indi-
viduality which had made Kalin so precious.

"Earl?"

"Nothing." The past was dead and ghosts should be left in
peace. Now, at this moment, only Ysanne was real. The
woman and the ship and the dangers they faced.

"I was thinking," she said. "About you and Maynard. I
thought you'd relied on luck to avoid getting hurt but now I
know better. You planned the whole thing from the very beginning. Watched and waited and moved when the time was
right. And, by God, how you moved! I've never seen anyone
so fast."

"It's over. Forget it."

"Aren't you curious? About him and me?"

"No."

Her hand tensed on his chest then relaxed. In the light she
looked wild, barbaric. An animal yet to be tamed, broken,
fitted with a yoke. She had come to him with an unabashed
directness and his response had matched her own.

"You're different," she mused. "From the very first moment we met I recognized that. We're two of a kind. What
you want you take. What you need you go after. Like me.
You can understand how it is; to see something and know
you must have it. *Must* have it. Once, when I was very
young, I saw a kalifox. It had fur which changed color in different lights and I wanted it. I wanted it so bad I hunted it
for seven weeks. I chased it over the plains and into the hills
and up into the snow and never gave it rest. I caught it in the
end."

"Did you enjoy the fur?"

"We both enjoyed it." She laughed with a soft amusement.
"I didn't kill it, Earl. I fed it and kept it for a pet until winter
came and it ran off to mate. I used to hear it barking from
the hills at night and, sometimes, I would bark back." She
snuggled a little closer. "Can you understand that?"

"Yes."

"Did you ever have a pet? On Earth, Earl? Did you?"

There had been no time for pets, no time for softness of
any kind. To catch an animal was to gain a meal and to feed
one was to invite starvation. Trust, love, affection, generos-
ity—all were luxuries he'd never known.

She seemed to sense this and she didn't press the question, talking instead of her own world.

"You'd like Manita, Earl. We live simple lives close to nature. Hunting, fishing, growing crops. No one tells another what to do. There are no pressures. A man doesn't have to prove himself. To live. To share. To help when help is needed."

"But you left."

"I said we lived simple lives not that we are ignorant. To keep what we have we must be as educated as those who might want to take it from us. So I learned. I was always good at finding my way around and it was natural I should become a navigator. I like it so I do it. When I stop liking it I do something else."

"Like hunting down a legend?"

"Of course. But it isn't that to you, is it? It's real and you want to go back home." Her tone gentled. "At times I feel the same. I remember the open plains and the hills and the nights when the sky glowed with stars. The meetings and pairings and the fun. The hunts, too, and the fishing, but most of all, I think, the freedom. That's when I begin to get restless."

"And move?"

"Yes."

"And when you stop liking what you're doing now?"

She said, "What you're really saying is what happens when I stop liking you. Isn't it obvious? We stop being lovers. We stop being companions. You want more?"

"I wasn't talking about us. I'm talking about our partnership. Does that end too?"

For a long moment she stared at him then, smiling, she said, "Earl, you fool, for us there'll be no ending. We'll go on until we find a new beginning. Then, maybe, you'll go running into the hills and, at night, I'll hear you barking."

"And will you bark back?"

"Maybe. That's for you to guess." She grew serious. "Don't worry, Earl, I'm no quitter. Once I start a thing I see it through. If Earth exists we'll find it."

"It exists."

"Then we'll find it." She stretched like a cat on the soft comfort of the bed. "Now kiss me before I go and check the controls."

Maynard's death had robbed the *Moira* of experience command. Seated in the big control chair Dumarest checke the instruments and studied the screens, going through routine which he had learned from service with various free traders, knowing it wasn't enough. To stand a temporar watch to relieve a tired captain was a different matter fron accepting the full responsibility of a ship and all it contained.

As yet they had been lucky. Space was clear and the auto matics capable of maintaining flight and safety, but space wa also deceptive and odd vortexes of energy lay in unexpected places. Swirling maelstroms of force could take a ship and rip it apart with opposed energies. Nodes held within their para meters the fury of dying suns. In these areas the instrument couldn't be trusted and only an experienced hand and eye could guide a ship on a safe route.

Experience Damarest lacked and he knew it.

"Earl?" Ysanne spoke from the intercom. "How is it going?"

"All right as yet. Are we on course?"

"The same as I set. Barely any deviation."

Proof of the superior efficiency of the *Moira*'s equipment but enough to have missed their target had it been distant.

"Change," ordered Dumarest. "Set a new course."

"To where?"

"Take your pick. I want a random pattern to throw off any pursuit."

"From whom? We took care of that other ship."

"Just do it."

This precaution could be unnecessary but there could always have been a third vessel which had remained unseen or which had arrived just after they had left. A ship could be following them with its sensors picking up the spatial disturbance left by their passage.

Such a command decision was a part of a captain's duties. As it was his job to oversee the general running of the ship and crew. To insure that there were correct supplies, fuel for the engines, air for the tanks. To delegate authority but never to be careless. No matter what happened to a ship; in the end only one person alone was responsible.

Craig reported from the intercom, "Generator's showing

signs of mounting inefficiency, Earl. I'd like to strip it down and monitor the coils."

"Have you replacements?"

"No. We were due for a refit but Pendance had to act in a hurry."

A decision was needed and Dumarest made it. "Leave things as they are for now. Checking will take time and the gain needn't be worth it. Let me know if the condition gets worse."

"As you say, Earl."

As the voice died an alarm flashed red, the glow holding for a long moment before the ruby turned green. A node of potential danger had been spotted by the sensors and avoided by the computer guidance system.

"Relax," said Ysanne from behind the chair. "Those lights will send you crazy if you stare at them long enough. That was Maynard's trouble. He couldn't trust the machines and ended by doubting himself." She moved so as to stand to one side, the braids of her hair reflecting the winking telltales in oily shimmers. "I've fed the course changes into the system. Three at varying angles and different periods. After the last we head to where we're going."

"Sorkendo?"

She betrayed her surprise. "How did you know we came from Sorkendo?"

"Why go back there?"

"Pendance has funds stashed away in the Homtage Bank and I figured we could get them. Land and claim he was dead and use them for a refit and supplies."

Dumarest said, "Were you checked in at the bank as a full crew-partner? Was Craig?"

"I wasn't and I'm sure Jed wasn't either. Does it matter? They know we're both a part of the *Moira*'s crew."

"It doesn't signify. Crews have been known to mutiny. A smart captain doesn't make it easy for them to gain any benefit from it."

"Maynard, then?" She frowned as she remembered. "Damn! We cycled him through the lock. We should have taken his hands first and used his prints to authenticate a deposition as to our right to claim."

The very suggestion revealed her lack of knowledge in certain areas.

"They wouldn't have accepted it," said Dumarest. "You aren't the first to have thought of that. In any case Pendance had probably radioed the bank to freeze his account."

"Of course! Why didn't I think of that?" She threw back her braids with an impatient gesture. "You'd have done better to have killed him, Earl. Well, if we can't go to Sorkendo, where else?"

To where the Cyclan wouldn't be waiting and they could find a captain willing to work for nothing but a promise. A world on which they could ready the *Moira* for a long journey—and to find it soon!

There was a subtle beauty in madness. An insidious attraction which manifested itself in the fabrication of complex logic which built alien worlds from accepted premises and realms of enticing fantasy from minor speculations.

Was this the root of the contamination?

Seated in his chair, alone in his office, Elge sensed rather than heard the swift interplay of minds honed and sharpened to a razor's edge. These intelligences had had centuries in which to ponder over abstract ideas, to create worlds based on adaptations of those concepts, to crystalize them into a variety of concrete wholes.

And that was the beauty of it. Not just one rigid universe beset by harsh disciplines but a plethora, each different from the other, each with its own basic logic. A game in which, like gods, the freed minds of old cybers had created worlds and planets and galaxies as they willed. Not *like* gods—they had *been* gods, each cyber in the world of his making the only true deity.

The recording ended and for a long moment Elge sat motionless in his chair. Had he and Nequal before him been guilty of a heinous crime? The recording had been taken from brains since destroyed. Minds judged to be insane and erased for fear of future contamination. But what if the apparent sickness had been the result of a natural progression? The next step in the evolutionary scale?

Elge had considered this possibility before. A mind, like a body, could grow and mature, develop like a child into a man. To progress from the fear-ridden, superstition-poisoned mentality of an aboriginal savage to the calculating intellect of a being able to recognize the stars for what they were, demons and ghosts for the nonsense they represented, the awe of the unknown for the ignorance it personified.

A normal man could do that contaminated as he was with destructive emotions. A cyber was superior to a normal man, free as he was from distorting glandular exudations. And, as a cyber to a man—the developed brains?

Even if that were so there had been no crime. Life was the cheapest thing in the universe and, though some had been destroyed, others would follow if the theory was correct. And would the development end there? Elge remembered the demonstration and the massive arm of the robot which had crushed the brain controlling it. It would be suicide if the mind had been aware of what was happening and what it was doing. But if it had been aware, and there was no doubt that was the case, could it have been not suicide but release?—the intelligence finally freed of the last vestige of hampering flesh so as to soar into the limitless regions of the universe?

Such speculation held endless connotations and opened vistas of entrancing complexity which a century of uninterrupted thought would only begin to comprehend.

Could the intelligence survive once the brain had been destroyed? The mind was not the organ—that much had been proved long ago. The ego, the self, was the product of an electromagnetic potential which could be plotted and measured and set down in graphs and wavering lines. Could be caught by machines which emulated telepathy as the recordings demonstrated.

And a world of the mind, to that mind, was as real as any other.

For a moment his senses swam and Elge straightened, one hand reaching toward the recorder to play again the trapped emissions of now-dead brains. Or brains which even now were enjoying true release. Freed from the prisons in which, all unwittingly, they had been placed.

His hand halted as the door opened and Jarvet entered the room, a folder beneath his arm.

"Master!" He placed the folder on the desk and glanced at the apparatus recently installed. "The latest report from Cyber Vire."

"Leave it."

"Yes, Master. The Council has studied the report and i would be best to bring your information up to date."

A warning? Elge glanced at the aide then at the folder. Engrossed with the recordings, he had mischanneled his energies and recognized the error. Time had been lost which should have been put to better use. A matter of minutes only, perhaps, but there could be no excuse for inefficiency.

He reached for the file and began to scan the contents.

Lim was dead and Vire had failed. The *Saito* had vaporized and all within it—Lim's pyre and one he had merited by his stupidity. Vire was not wholly to blame and yet the tools he had chosen reflected on his ability.

"Time was a matter of prime importance," said Jarvet as Elge put down the final sheet. "He contacted agents on Sorkendo while in transit and arranged for a military-type operation. One which, as we now know, failed."

That failure left the cyber in a damaged vessel, the mercenaries dead or stranded, their own ship taken by the man they had been engaged to capture.

Where was he now?

Correction—where would he be? And when?

Elge looked again at the report. As yet Vire had made only radio contact with Pendance and it would take time before his ship could reach Zabul. The result for which Dumarest had planned.

How to locate him in the immensity of space?

A man, using available transportation, was restricted to certain definable areas of operation. He could only go where ships were available to take him. Even if he adopted a random path it could never wholly be that because, always, his choices were limited. But now Dumarest was in his own vessel and could go where he pleased.

At least so it seemed, but Elge knew better.

Paper moved beneath his hand as he checked certain data. Vire had been thorough in his questioning of Pendance and his men. Facts; details as to supplies carried by the *Moira*, the temperament of the crew, the state of the vessel itself—all helping to build an overall picture.

The faulty generator would slow the ship and need repairing. Fuel was low. Of the crew Maynard had emotional difficulties which could lead to a confrontation if the woman was areless. The engineer, while skilled, would be of little use outside his field.

To operate the ship Dumarest would need men, money and material.

And those needs could drive him into a trap.

CHAPTER NINE

Ysanne said, "Millett, Earl, or Emney. Either will do but you'll have to decide now so I can set the new course. Even as it is we'll be pushing things to the limit."

She sat in the chart room, almanacs at her side, the chamber filled with the flash and winks from the instruments, the pungent odor of her perfume, which was in keeping with the barbaric dress she wore: leather decorated with painted symbols, the skirt fringed and falling to her knees. The belt hugging her waist was broad, beaded, the buckle massive.

She seemed a savage seated in the middle of modern technology, hair and skin illuminated by the glow of telltales and registers. It was easy to imagine her squatting before an open fire, tearing at half-cooked meat with her strong teeth, face and hands smeared with grease and stained with smoke. A child of nature, now over-tired and short on patience.

"Earl?"

A choice and a decision he had to make but one he didn't like. The choice was too limited, the decision too predictable.

"Millett is favorite by a hair," she said. "Good yards and facilities. We could raise a loan or charter the ship to cover the cost of fees and generator-parts. Emney is more isolated but could do the job and we'd have no trouble eating. The place is lousy with game."

"You know it?"

"I've been there." She volunteered no further information. Instead, as if reading his mind, she said, "You aren't happy with either. Why? Afraid of Pendance?"

98

Pendance was the least of his worries; the man would be dead by now if Volodya had any sense. But she had provided a reason he could use.

"He could have friends who'd recognize the *Moira* and get curious. They might even decide to take over and we aren't strong enough to safeguard the ship. Are you sure there's no other choice?"

"There's always a choice. We could drift until we're forgotten and thought dead. We could try to reach the Puchon or Venner's Twin—good worlds if you can breathe chlorine. We could even try praying for a miracle—one which will give us fuel and a new generator and supplies."

"I'm serious."

"So am I." Her gesture embraced the instruments, the almanacs and navigational tables, the charts. "Facts, Earl. I have to deal in facts and they are against us. We aren't free agents. That damned generator makes us prisoners of the equations and we can only go so far. So which is it to be? Millett or Emney?"

The decision was reached through fatigue but absolved her of further strain. Now the burden was his and she could rest and close her eyes and remember the touch of cool winds on her face and hair as she ran over rolling plains to where the fires of the evening meeting already shone like ruby stars beneath their thin columns of smoke.

That moment of illusory comfort was lost as he said, harshly, "You're falling down on the job. You boasted you were the best navigator in space but this is a hell of a way to prove it. Maybe I should ask Craig to take over."

Her eyes opened, flaring with the anger he'd deliberately aroused; rage washed her brain clear of dulling fatigue even as it thinned her lips.

"Earl! You—"

"Think again," he snapped, giving her no time to protest. "And stop trying to play it safe. Drift, you said, well, why not? Maybe we could use a force-current or magnetic flow to help stretch the fuel. Damn it, woman, use your imagination!"

She said tightly, "Pendance was a bastard—don't try to be a bigger one."

"Or?" He saw the movement of her hand and caught her wrist as her fingers touched the bright metal of her buckle.

"You'll kill me, is that it? He gripped the metal and pulled and looked at the blade which shone in his hand. Short, with a double-edge and a wicked point. A stabbing blade with the buckle acting as a grip. "Have you ever used this?"

"You want a demonstration?"

Dumarest shook his head and slid the blade back into the belt. Rising, he stepped back and away from the woman, watchful, ready to act if her rage overpowered her. She sat where he had left her, seething, fighting for control. A wrong word and, like the innate savage she was, she would explode into a mindless, berserker fury.

At the door he said, "Get back to work. Use that skill you boasted of. Forget those worlds you mentioned and find alternatives. And do it soon!"

"Go to hell!"

"Do it!" She recoiled as he stepped toward her, his face a mask of barbaric cruelty as ugly as his voice. "Do it or, by God, you'll learn what a real bastard can be!"

Outside he strode down the corridor, fighting to control the anger which had started as pretense and edged into the real. Too much depended on the woman for him to be gentle. Strong herself she respected only a greater strength; a trait which could have drawn her to Pendance mistaking the slaver's viciousness for the attribute she admired.

Reaching the captain's cabin Dumarest entered and looked around, seeing the whips, the electronic scourges, the mementoes of his career. The cabinet held ornate finery and a box of assorted rings and gems of price. Spoils he could use as he could the bottle of rare brandy and the vials of stimulating drugs. Opening the spirit, he added the contents of a vial, shook the mixture and went in search of the engineer.

Craig was lying asleep on the cot he kept in the engine room, lost in a nightmare in which he lay at the edge of a turbulent sea wreathed in hampering weed and with crabs tearing at his face. Cruel pincers ripped and stung and shed his blood to be lapped by slimed things which reared from the sand.

Looking down at him Dumarest saw the restless twitching of the eyeballs beneath their lids. Sweat dewed the scarred face and edged the spikes of hair. Lines had dug their way into the corners of the eyes and the expanse of the forehead betraying marks of age as was the flaccid skin beneath the jaw, the mottled blotches marring the hands. The man was too old to hope for a better berth, content to ride with slavers, to be treated like a dog. He needed a carrot as Ysanne needed a whip.

He shuddered awake as Dumarest touched his shoulder.

"God! I thought—God!" Sleeping while on duty, taken unawares—what would Pendance have done? Then he saw the tall figure standing at his side with the bottle in his hand. "I dropped off," he said quickly. "Just to take a short nap. The instruments were beginning to blur."

Excuses Dumarest didn't need. He said, gently, "You needed a rest, Jed, and were wise enough to take it. A tired brain can make mistakes and you're the only engineer around. Like a drink?" He lifted the bottle. "Mind sharing the neck?"

Craig shook his head, rising to stand beside Dumarest as he tilted the bottle, neck to his mouth, throat working as he pretended to drink.

"Here!"

"Thanks!" Craig's own drink was real and he felt the warm comfort of the alcohol as it hit his stomach, the stimulation of the drugs it contained which banished his nagging fatigue. "We got a destination yet?"

"Ysanne's working on it."

"A smart girl. The kind I could have gone for if I were younger and had the kind of face a woman could bear to look at. It was never good but Pendance made it worse. Well, the bastard got what was coming."

Dumarest said, "Those scars can be fixed."

"Sure. With money."

"You'll get money. We'll all get it. A fortune." Dumarest held out the bottle. "Have another drink."

Craig nodded his thanks and swallowed and said, "You understand, Earl. You've known what it is to be short and stranded and glad to take anything as long as you can eat. I'm a good engineer. I can strip and assemble a generator, tune it too, there's not many can do that without the right equipment."

"I believe you," said Dumarest. "I guess we're lucky to have you. Ysanne and I, that is. Our lives are in your hands. Think we can make it?"

"I wish I knew." Craig gestured to the console, the instruments it carried. "The synch-variation is getting wilder and I don't know how much longer it will stay within tolerance. It could strike a balance, but if it doesn't and the generator goes—" He broke off, shrugging. "I guess you know what'll happen then."

The Erhaft field would collapse to leave the *Moira* drifting in space at sub-light velocity. Long before it could reach a planet they could all be dead.

Dumarest said, "I expect you've thought of fixing a monitor to cut the field if the variation gets too far out of line?"

"I was about to do that."

"Good. One with a mutual override? How long will it take?"

"Not long. It's mostly a matter of registers and cut-outs. Say a couple of hours. I'll have to cut the drive to do it though. When do you want me to start?"

"As soon as you're ready. Can you manage on your own?"

"Sure, but you could leave me the bottle."

Dumarest lifted it, checking the contents. More and the engineer would have had too much. "Later," he said. "I'll save it until you've finished."

Back in the control room Dumarest took his place in the big chair, letting his head fall back against the padding, looking at the screens with their patterns of stars, the instruments, the glowing telltales. As normal the room was in gloom, the lights bright, hypnotic in their shifting flickers.

Captains rarely stood watch alone. Usually there was someone with them, the second in command, the chief engineer, the navigator, a junior officer. A human presence to ease the strain of concentration as well as to provide a second pair of eyes and a brain to monitor the messages the instruments delivered.

To be alone was to be enclosed in a surrogate womb, warm, comfortable, isolated, entranced by endless vistas of space.

"Earl!" Dumarest jerked as Craig's voice came from the intercom. He had been drifting on the edge of sleep, bemused by the lights, the repetitive pulse of a glaring ruby eye on a piece of unfamiliar apparatus. "Ready to cut drive now."

"A moment." Dumarest checked the systems and found no trace of ethereal danger. "Go ahead."

A moment later the stars flickered as the instruments flared. An alarm sounded, dying as he touched a control, lights shifting as the ship's systems adjusted to the new conditions. Now the *Moira* was helpless before the impact of interstellar forces; the shifts and eddies of spatial disturbances which eroded planetoids, disintegrated the detritus of broken worlds, turned hapless vessels into things of abstract sculpture.

Before him the ruby light blazed with a new, eye-searing intensity and looking at it Dumarest knew what it had to be.

A radio beacon.

Something in space was calling for help.

"It's a ship! Earl! It's a ship!" Ysanne leaned close, previous animosity long forgotten in the excitement of the chase, eyes glistening with reflected light as she stared at the shape swelling larger in the screens. Slow down, Earl! Slower!"

The shape steadied as he obeyed, seeming to move as the *Moira* came to relative rest. A craft after the general pattern of their own, the hull blotched with markings.

"The *Galya*," said Craig as he joined them in the control room. "Small, maybe a private, adapted to carry extra cargo." He read the symbols and design with practiced ease. "Not drifting for long by the look of her. There'd be more attrition of the plates if she had. Any idea as to where she's from?"

"No." There had been no answer to their signals. Dumarest added, "We'd best try direct laser contact. That beacon's automatic and the normal radio could be broken. Ten minutes, Jed?"

It took fifteen before Dumarest, suited, saw the hatch open and the *Galya* framed in the aperture. He lifted the communication-laser in gloved hands, aimed, fired the beam and spoke into the connected microphone.

"Calling the *Galya*. *Moira* calling the *Galya*. We picked up your signal. Answer if you can."

He received vibrations carried as electronic pulses by the beam of the laser, impinging on the hull and being translated back into vibration. These harmonics repeated his voice within the ship's structure.

"Answer if you can. Flash a light. Show a signal. Respond. Respond!"

Again the wait, the silence.

"Dead," said Craig. "They must all be dead."

Lying stark and withered or too ill to move. Starved or de-hydrated, listening to the voice of rescue but unable to make the one sign which would bring it in time. Not, perhaps, even recognizing his voice for what it was.

An emergency radio beacon was the last, desperate effort anyone stranded in space could make. The odds against it being picked up were astronomical. The chance that, even if it was received, a ship would break its journey to make a tedious search was almost as slim. Only the hope of a reward would encourage anyone to try.

"Salvage," muttered Craig. "The kind a man dreams about. All out there for the taking—and we've no way to get it to a market. What do we do, Earl?"

"Go and investigate," said Dumarest. "But I'll go alone."

He heard a keening as he crossed the gap between the ships; a thin, wailing echo which lifted to fade and die as if a crying child had been suddenly snatched far distant at high velocity. The sound seemed to originate within his brain, created by electronic impulses from surging particles of radiation, riding a spatial wind or circling and gaining momentum as they spun in the magnetic flux which could swell to become the heart of a vortex or the twisting complex of a warp.

A danger sign he ignored as the *Galya* grew large before him.

The hull slapped against his boots and he swayed before inching over the rounded plates to where the lock rested toward the rear. It was sealed but there was an emergency trip on which he rested his hand.

To Ysanne he said, "Anything?"

"Nothing, Earl. It's still as dead as before." Her tone carried a note of anxiety. "The instruments register a growing nexus of undisciplined energy. We're close to a decaying vortex and there could be a transference of energy potential. If so there could be a danger of a local storm."

"Remote or immediate?"

"You've got time," she said. "But don't waste any. Be careful—I want you back."

The trip moved beneath his hand and the lock gaped open. Releasing his safety line he jammed it against the hull, the gekko-pad holding it fast. Inside the lock he paused for a moment then thumbed the mechanism. Rotated inside he stepped from the lock into the hold of the vessel.

It was as he had expected, matching the holds of a hundred other vessels he had known. A compartment half-filled with bales, some sacs lying to one side, the caskets designed for the transportation of beasts lined up beneath a cold, blue-white glow. The normal appearance of any trader working on a slender margin. The handler probably doubled as steward, there would be only one engineer, one navigator, a captain and his second in command. Even if, as Craig had suggested, the *Galya* was a private vessel, there would be no more.

Dumarest moved toward the engine room, opened the door and stared at a scene of devastation. The generator was ruined, nothing but a seared and fused mass of metal resting where it had been. To one side the burned body of a man lay in a pool of congealed blood, the fluid dried to a brown hardness. The blast which had caught him had seared his upper torso, turning his head into a knob of ash, his chest into a blackened crust through which showed the yellow of bare bone. His hands were gone, his arms past the elbows, and Dumarest guessed he had been leaning over the generator, touching it, when it had blown.

From the lower regions a corridor ran between cabins to the salon and control area. Light shone with a steady luminescence from plates set in the ceiling and dust reflected it in misty shimmers. A sure sign of air but Dumarest made no effort to open his helmet. The air could be breathable but contaminated.

A cabin door opened beneath the pressure of his hand and he saw an unmade bunk, some scattered clothing, a bottle lying on its side, a scatter of small, blue pills. The pillow carried long, dark hairs, and a woman's cosmetic kit rested on a shelf. Another held some toys, a heap of small garments, the portrait of a girl with wide eyes who clutched a furry pet.

In the third waited madness.

Dumarest saw the flicker of motion and threw himself backwards as steel whined through the air where he had stood. A long, curved blade shimmered like a mirror bathed in light, flashing as it sliced toward him, missing as he dodged, making a dull, flat sound as it bit deep into the edge of the door.

Bit and stuck as the man who wielded it screamed in maniacal fury.

He was tall, skeleton-thin, wearing soiled but ornate robes. His hair hung in a shoulder-length tangle from a peaked skull and his mouth, open, revealed filed teeth set with gems. The eyes were red, crusted, blotched with yellow.

His face belonged to a creature from delirium.

The flesh had left the contours of the bone and taken on a shape of its own, hanging in pendulous drippings and puffed protrusions as if the face had been made of wax and exposed to the softening influence of a fire. Or of a soft plastic bathed in the vapors of a corrosive acid.

"No!" he screamed. "You will not take me! The transformation is not yet complete. I will not yield to demons of torment. Die! Die!"

The sword came ripping from the door to lift and slash as Dumarest turned and ran down the corridor back to the hold. Hampered by his suit, restricted by the confines of the cabin and corridor, faced by a creature with insane strength and a sword which could slash through metal, he needed space in which to defend himself.

He reached in just in time, diving sideways as the blade whined through air, moving, searching for a weapon, seeing a pile of metal rods stacked beside a case together with the familiar bulk of an extinguisher.

Dumarest reached it as curved steel slashed a long opening in his suit, lifting it as the blade rose for another cut, ducked behind a case as it came down. A moment gained in which he slammed his head against the control and raised the extinguisher in time to block a slash which would have taken the head from his shoulders.

Foam spouted from the nozzle, caught the tormented face, the red, glaring eyes. Filled the mouth with its substance and coated arms and torso with clinging whiteness. The foam robbed the air of oxygen and sent the swordsman to his knees, blade falling, hands lifting as he fought to clear his mouth. The fight ended as the assailant slumped, sprawling, in the unmistakable posture of death.

CHAPTER TEN

The hold was silent save for the gushing whisper of air from his tanks, Ysanne's voice echoing urgently from the speakers.

"Earl! Earl, answer me! Is anything wrong? I heard odd noises. Earl!"

"Nothing's wrong." She had caught the sounds of combat carried via the diaphragms. He hurried on before she could demand explanations. "Everything's under control here. Can you move the *Moira* to make direct contact?"

"Maybe, but it wouldn't be wise. That storm I mentioned is building up into something serious. Direct contact means we increase our united mass and invite energy condensation."

"Do what you can. I want things easy for transfer."

"People? Goods?" A pause, then, "How's the generator?"

He left that question unanswered as he doffed the suit. Slashed, it was useless and if the air was contaminated he had already been exposed. Drawing his knife he stepped to where the swordsman lay sprawled and kicked aside the fallen blade. Thirty inches of polished steel, curved like the stamen of a flower, the hilt a continuation of the blade, made of wood elaborately carved. The guard was small, ornate, and from the pommel hung a tassle of yellow silk.

A weapon favored by the Akita of Sardo—had the *Galya* come from there?

Dumarest rested his left foot on the man's right wrist and, stopping over the figure, used the point of his knife to open an artery. The blood barely welled from the shallow gash, ly-

107

ing dark and turgid in the wound. A sure sign of death; that
was a precaution, as had been his silence as to the condition
of the generator. If Ysanne knew it had blown and was useless she might be tempted to leave him and run—take the
Moira to a close world, sell it and live soft on the proceeds.
Twice as soft if Craig was disposed of.

"Earl!" Her voice called from the speakers of the discarded
helmet. "Earl, answer me, damn you! Earl!"

The voice faded as he made his way back up the corridor,
ears strained, body alert, and he halted to lean against a
door. This cabin was empty but showed signs of hasty evacu-
ation; clothing scattered, some rings and vials of perfume lying on the floor. One had broken and the air held the
memory of a cloying scent.

In the next cabin he entered lay the body of a man.

He was dressed like the swordsman in an ornate robe, the
condition immaculate, the long hair braided and wound in a
topknot pierced with a spine of polished wood. His thin
hands rested on his chest, the fingers gripping a sword which
was the twin to the other. Cosmetics had turned his face into
a snarling mask of bestial fury, but beneath the paint it was
unravaged.

Next to him, on a small table, rested an empty glass containing the dregs of wine and a locket graced with a familiar
symbol. Dumarest looked at the grinning skull, at the glass,
then at the dead man. Suicide, but the painted face showed it
was not chosen because of any personal sense of disgrace.
The man had armed himself, painted himself for war—and
had died to combat enemies untouchable on a physical plane.

The rest of the cabins were deserted or locked as was the
salon, the control rooms. Dumarest returned to the hold and
picked up one of the metal bars. Back at the salon he
rammed it between the door and the jamb, heaved, stepped
back as it yielded.

At the table sat a ring of statues.

Men and women frozen in the midst of a game, cards in
their fingers, chips scattered on the baize. An old woman,
gems on her gnarled fingers, cosmetics on her raddled cheeks.
A younger woman at her side, hard-faced, hair cropped,
dressed in a quilted tunic, pants, calf-high boots. Two others
who could have been attendants. A man who had the appearance of a trader. Another who wore the robe of a monk.

The monk sat at the end of the table, cowl thrown back to reveal a face thin but not austere, as if he had seen too much of the harsh side of life; the poverty and deprivation, the disease, the hunger, the despair which stalked all worlds like a corroding miasma. A man who believed in a simple credo and was dedicated to a life of personal sacrifice, he wore no gems; ornaments could buy food for the hungry. He had no pride; that was a luxury beggars could not afford. He had nothing but the conviction that, one day, when all men could look at each other and say, *"There, but for the grace of God, go I!"* the millennium would have arrived.

He would never live to see it; men bred too fast and spread too quickly, but he would continue to do what he could to ease suffering where he found it. He and his fellows formed the Church of Universal Brotherhood.

Neither he nor the others had looked up when Dumarest had broken open the door. Lost in the magic of quick time, their metabolism slowed to far below normal, they had barely registered the incident. For them normal minutes were but seconds and before they could even see him he had gone.

At the control room Dumarest lifted the bar then, pausing, again tried the door. This time it swung open and he looked into the dim interior lit with the glow of signal lights, the blaze of stars from the screens.

In one of them the *Moira* loomed close, Ysanne's voice coming from a speaker, edged with sharp impatience.

"Respond, damn you! Calling the *Galya!* Calling the *Galya!* Signal if you can hear! Respond!"

Dumarest moved forward and touched a button. "All right, Ysanne, contact established."

"Earl! What—"

"Have Craig come over with a spare suit to collect what he needs." Alone she could never handle the *Moira.* "I'm in the control room with the captain." Dumarest looked inquiringly at the figure seated in the big chair. "Captain Andre Batrun. We're about to discuss terms of rescue."

Batrun was old, his face lined, his hair a neat crop of silver. He had spent his life in the cold reaches between the stars and now, ripe with experience, faced total ruin.

"Life," he mused. "What is it worth? Without it you have nothing, so, therefore, it must be worth all you possess."

He found this philosophy less than comforting and he took a pinch of snuff from an ornate box and dusted a few grains of the brown powder from his impeccable uniform. Watching him, Dumarest could guess his thoughts.

"Let's talk of salvage," he said. "Your generator is ruined and without it the *Galya* is useless. Which leaves your cargo and whatever else can be transferred."

"Agreed." Batrun made a small gesture. "I am not a man to expect another to burn atoms, break his journey and take risks for nothing. But I carry passengers and some of the cargo is theirs."

To be forfeited with all else they possessed if Dumarest insisted and they hoped for rescue. These details could be settled later; now he was curious as to what had happened.

"Madness," said Batrun. "Bad luck and, from what happened, sabotage. I'm carrying the Matriarch Su Posta and her party to Jourdan and we had trouble from the beginning. My handler fell sick with an infection which affected his brain and he ran amok. Three died before he could be restrained; then he broke free and headed for the generator. God knows what he intended but, apparently, he tried to open the casing and it blew." He nodded as he saw Dumarest's frown. "I agree. It shouldn't have done that and the only explanation I can think of is that it was booby-trapped in some way, perhaps with a device coupled to a timer which would have done the same job. He anticipated it, that's all."

"And?"

"What can you do when your ship is drifting?" Batrun took a pinch of snuff. "Each make their own arrangements."

Some to die quick and clean by their own hand. Others to settle into a routine, facing extinction as all creatures faced it—the only real difference being the sharpened awareness of time.

"The Akita?"

"A part of the matriarch's retinue. Bodyguards. The one who attacked you had been caught in the fringe of the blast when the generator went."

His flesh reacting to wild radiations, swelling in grotesque cancerous growths, the brain itself distorted to fill the universe with inimical foes.

Dumarest said, "He thought he was being transformed into

something wonderful. Well, now, maybe he is. Have you men to help with the transfer?"

"The steward and second engineer. The matriarch might let you use some of her people."

Su Posta was no longer a statue. The drug had been neutralized and she and the others now lived on normal time. She looked up as Dumarest entered her cabin, her eyes hard, imperious. When she spoke her voice held the arrogance of one long accustomed to implicit obedience.

"How long will it be before we are on our way?"

"Not long, my lady."

"That is not answering the question!"

He said quietly, "There are matters to be attended to and details to be arranged. I assure you that—"

"You will be paid," she snapped. "I do not wish to haggle."

"How many are in your retinue?"

"Myself, my granddaughter, two attendants, her governess and, yes, you can include the monk." Her voice took on a new asperity. "Are you intending to charge by the head?"

"I was thinking of transfer. We cannot make direct contact and so will have to transship in sacs. There is nothing to worry about but it can be a little frightening to those inexperienced. A child, say, or—"

"An old woman?"

"Yes, my lady. Some old women."

"But I am not one of them." The concept was almost amusing. She, the Matriarch of Jourdan, afraid! "The governess will accompany my granddaughter, I shall travel alone. The rest can make their own arrangements." Her gesture dismissed them as being of no importance. "Where are you bound?" She did not wait for an answer. "You will take us to Jourdan."

"Perhaps, my lady."

She blinked at his answer and stared at him with sharpened interest. Tall, hard—the way she had liked her men when younger. How she still liked them even if only to look at and keep warm old memories. Figures which held the attribute she so admired, the determination of purpose which was her own strength. But even admiration had to yield to the necessity of being obeyed.

She said, bluntly, "That was an order."

Dumarest was equally blunt. "One you are in no position to give. I command the *Moira*."

"Must I remind you who I am?"

"I know who you are, my lady. I also know what you are at this present time."

"A person at your mercy, it seems." Her tone was bitter. "Have you come to gloat?"

"I came to ask the use of some of your people to help in the transfer." He added, "The quicker it's done the sooner we can be on our way."

"To Jourdan." It was not a question. "Take me to Jourdan and you will be highly rewarded." Her eyes, deep-set, cold, watchful as those of a snake, searched his face. "Very highly rewarded. You have my word on that."

"Thank you, my lady," said Dumarest. "But I'd prefer it in writing."

Batrun's engineer was a woman, Olga Wenzer, short, brown, her hair grizzled. She watched Craig's deft movements and nodded, recognizing his ability and taking second place.

To Dumarest she said, "I can fill in if needed but you've got a good man there. How about a handler or a steward?"

"Shandhar is carrying on as that."

"A handler, then. Ben's a good steward." She added, "I guess he's glad of the berth. I know I would be."

"I can't pay you."

"You already have. We'd be dead if it weren't for you. A handler, then?"

Dumarest nodded and watched as she walked away to take up her duties. A new member of the crew and a new responsibility to add to the rest. Batrun and the steward and the passengers. One came running toward him as he headed toward the control room; a small bundle of furious energy which threw herself at him to be caught up in his arms and lifted high.

"Lucita!" Her governess shook her head in mock reproof as Dumarest tossed the little girl and set her squealing with laughter. "You spoil her, Earl. The future Matriarch of Jourdan should not be spoiled."

"She's young," said Dumarest. "And very beautiful." This last to the girl herself. "Will you make a good ruler? One who is kind and generous and who knows the meaning of mercy? Of course you will. Hungry? Then why not go and find Olga and ask her to ask Ben to find you something nice to eat? Want to go?"

She nodded, beaming.

"Then go!" He set her on her feet and watched her as she raced away and turned to see the governess looking at him with a strange expression. "Something wrong?"

"No. No it's just that—" She broke off, shaking her head. "You surprise me a little. I would never have thought you to love children."

"Why not?"

Because he looked too hard, too self-centered and because he commanded a ship which was too like a slaver for coincidence. Helga, the girl's bodyguard, relayed these facts and she should know. And yet, remembering how he had won Lucita's heart, she began to have doubts.

Batrun was in the control room, Ysanne at his side. Together they checked the instruments, while in the screens the bulk of the *Galya* drifted away, driven by the reaction of air released from its tanks. The hull shimmered with spots and twinkles of brightness; a growing scintillation which held a fascinating beauty but which warned of mounting danger.

"The nexus is centering," said Ysanne. "The hulls are acting as magnets and the potential is nearing the lower critical level. If we're going we'd better get started."

Batrun said, "We need to plot a course which will avoid the nexus but take advantage of the peripheral swirl. Can you cut in analogue filters?"

"Sure." Ysanne reached for the controls. "There!"

Space changed, became a thing of streaming colors, stabbing shafts and waves of brilliance. Energy, invisible to the eye, translated into visual light. Glowing masses which moved to coalesce and form nodes and swirls and peaks of wild forces. Radiation, particles of atoms, small furies which accumulated to equal the potential energy contained in a sun.

Dangers swept away from planetary systems by the solar wind, gathering in interstellar space to form a series of destructive hazards.

Dumarest said, "Captain!"

"What is it?" Batrun turned then, remembering, shook his head. "I'm sorry. Old habits die hard. I'm not the captain."

"You could be. I've spoken to the others about it. Ysanne

and Craig share partnership with me—you may have heard about it." Ysanne's nod confirmed he had. "You've lost your command but you could get another if you're interested. Are you?"

A question put out of courtesy and Batrun could appreciate the consideration. Few captains survived the loss of a command—death was cleaner than to hang about fields after berths which didn't exist. He was too old to hope for a ship, too poor to buy a part in one, too proud to beg.

"Equal shares," said Dumarest. "And I'm not being generous. You'll earn it—and there's a condition."

"To find Earth," said Batrun. "I know." His eyes moved to the woman. "And after?"

"Does it matter?"

"To me—no." Batrun took snuff, his hand shaking a little as he lifted the powder to his nostrils. "I'd go to hell for the sake of a command. You see, I am honest."

And skilled, as he demonstrated after he had taken his place in the big chair, hands moving as if to caress the padding as he settled in his new environment.

"Engineer?" He listened to Craig's report on the generator. "Navigator?"

"Course selected for Jourdan, Captain." Ysanne matched his formality. "Three-stage flight pattern. First to operate within five seconds from activation."

"Check. Mark!"

Dumarest watched, counting, the blue cocoon of the Erhaft field appearing to envelop them in its protective shimmer as, in the screens, the *Galya* suddenly crumpled to twisted ruin.

CHAPTER ELEVEN

Ysolto Mbushia looked at the paper and thoughtfully pursed his lips, one hand lifting, the fingers tracing the pattern of ritual scars which stood livid on his cheeks.

"Well, now," he said. "I'm not sure."

"Why the doubt? The signature's good, isn't it?"

"How would I know?" The Hausi looked at Dumarest and lifted his shoulders in a shrug. "The Matriarch Su Posta could have written this or someone could have done it for her. Signed it too. You see the difficulty?"

"The signature's been countersigned." Dumarest pointed. "And thumbprinted. And witnessed by a monk. Brother Vezey. He was with the matriarch's retinue."

"So?"

"You don't know the monk's handwriting either. Nor the thumbprint. I understand. But I'm not asking you to give me cash over the counter. Just hold it, verify it and collect. Pay me only when it's been cleared." Then, as the Hausi continued to hesitate, Dumarest added, "Naturally there'll be a commission. Ten percent?"

"The usual is twenty."

"Fifteen and you can handle our supplies and repairs. A deal?"

The Hausi nodded and smiled. "A deal, my friend. To be sealed in wine. Here, on Jourdan, we have our traditions. A moment if you please while I fetch the bottle."

"And a copy of the promissory note," reminded Dumarest.

"Together with your receipt and statement as to the agreed commission."

"You don't trust me?"

"Yes," said Dumarest. A Hausi did not lie. "I trust you but I have partners and they don't trust me. What about that wine?"

It was sweet, cool, tasting of mint and honey and he savored it as he leaned with his back against the counter. Through the open door of the agency he could see the field, the bulk of the *Moira* together with other vessels. A busy field and an economically viable world if the ranked warehouses were anything to go by. Even as he watched, a line of carts appeared, low trailers drawn by sweating men each loaded with bulging sacks.

"Choum," said the Hausi. "A high-protein food destined for the mines on Calvardopolis. A short run and little profit but better than nothing if your ship's lying idle. If you're interested I could arrange the load."

Dumarest shook his head; the *Moira* was grounded until it could be repaired. He watched as the men dragged their loads closer to the warehouse. The whips of overseers made spiteful, cracking sounds.

"Vagrants," said Mbushia. "Debtors and petty criminals working off their sentences on work gangs." He sipped at his wine. "Forgers lose their hands."

"Thinking of that note?" Dumarest finished his wine and set down the glass. "Forget it if it bothers you. I'll try somewhere else. Maybe the palace itself. The journey's worth ten percent."

"We agreed on fifteen."

"So we did." Dumarest met the agent's eyes. "And it's genuine. Maybe I should see a doctor." He joined the other's laughter, then, "How long?"

"A little while. The matriarch isn't a quick payer and it might be best to discount the note. How low will you go?"

"Face value or nothing—I'm not that stupid. Not yet."

Outside Dumarest looked up at the sky and felt the warmth of the sun. It felt good, as did the touch of wind on his face, the grit of dirt beneath his boots. Space was too cold, too hostile. There was nowhere to hide and nothing soft to see. Nothing green like the leaf he pulled from a shrub to crush and lift to his nostrils and smell. No water like that which came gushing from a fountain to fill the air with musical tinklings. Ships were traps from which there could be no escape and space was an all-enveloping enemy.

Fantasies but he was glad the journey was over. It had taken too long and would have been impossible without the fuel salvaged from the *Galya*. Only that and Batrun's skill had enabled them to use the currents and nurse the generator until finally settling on solid ground. The generator was ruined and would have to be replaced—the matriarch's reward would cover it.

She had gone together with her retinue; the small child, the governess, the bodyguard, the attendants, the monk. The man who had looked like a trader had been an advocate and he had gone too. So had Craig, hunting a new generator. Olga had gone with him and Shandhar had left to see about supplies. Only Ysanne and Batrun remained.

"Earl!" She waved to him as he entered the salon. Batrun was with her, papers spread between them, and Dumarest caught a glimpse of navigational symbols; lines, zones, waves, the tools of her trade. "Come and sit with us. Andre's been telling me some of the things he learned as a boy working the Chelham Ridge. You know it? It's an area where if you spit you'd splash a dozen worlds. Full of opposed gravities, magnetic fluxes, the works. You can head for one place and wind up at another. Turn almost a full circle. Right, Andre?"

He nodded, looking at Dumarest.

"Like a maze," she said. "Like threading a needle through a head of cabbage. It goes in but you don't know where the hell it's coming out. Fun, eh? Good fun, Earl. Damned good fun. Right?"

She talked too fast and her eyes were too bright and he guessed she'd been drinking but wasn't yet wholly drunk. Just enough for tensions to have eased and emotion to be vented in a flurry of words. A compensation too, perhaps, for Batrun's having shown her how relatively inexperienced she really was.

"I'll get some coffee, Earl," he said, rising. "I think Ysanne may have celebrated our landing with a little too much enthusiasm."

"I can't drink," she said. "Is that what you're saying? Nobody from Manito can drink. We've more sense than to rot our guts with poison. When we want kicks we chew weed or change lovers or have a fight. You know, Earl, that's an idea. Maybe we should have a fight. Winner take all, right? Winner takes all."

"What have we got? A broken down ship, some supplies, some cargo still to be turned into cash."

"And a promise, Earl. That old bag should be grateful."

"Maybe." Dumarest looked up as Batrun returned. He carried a steaming pot and a vial of tablets. "Sobup pills," he explained. "She must have got the wine from Shandhar. Here." He offered her two with a cup of coffee. "Take these and you'll soon feel better."

A promise fulfilled as she set down her empty cup and sat blinking at the scattered papers.

"A little wine," she said, "and your brains take wings. Now I know why we don't drink back home. How the hell do you manage it, Earl?"

"Practice." He looked at the papers. "Apart from the lesson what's been happening?"

"We talked," she said. "I suggested changing the name of the ship. I don't like the *Moira*. It was Pendance's choice and I want to forget that bastard." Glancing at Batrun she said, "Why not the *Galya*?"

"No!" He softened the rejection. "No, I'd rather not. For me there could only ever be one *Galya*. But, in view of our search, why not the *Erce*?"

"*Erce*?" Ysanne thought about it. "An odd name but why not? Earl?"

He said, "Where did you hear it, Andre?"

"Does it matter?" Ysanne was impatient. "It's a name. Erce." She shook her head. "One you wouldn't forget in a hurry. What does it mean?"

"Earth," said Batrun. "It's another name for Earth. You couldn't call a ship that, could you? Not Earth. And not Terra either. Strange how old names lose their meaning. Earth is ground or dirt and we still use it in that connection. As we do terra—terrain. But Erce?"

Dumarest said, again, "Andre—where did you hear it?"

"From a book, I think. Yes, it had to be that." He saw Dumarest's expression and continued. "Most of a captain's job is to wait. To stand watch and do nothing but wait and fight boredom. Some do it with drugs, others with symbiotes; I used books—old ones, mostly, dealing with legends and myths. Did you know that Bonanza actually exists? That Eden was a real world and you can visit Heaven any time you want? They call it Haveen now but it has to be the same planet. But to be more specific. Erce was a term used in a wider sense than a name. Think of it not as meaning just Earth but as Mother Earth—you see the difference?"

"Mother Earth," she said. "Erce."

"There are other names we could use and all with the same vague origins. Selene, for example. Now that is assumed to be a goddess and she is worshipped on Marl. Each girl, when reaching puberty, must go into the sacred environs there to submit herself to any who ask. Man or woman, it makes no difference, she has to submit to their demand. They, in turn, make a donation to the priestesses. Of course there are ways to avoid an unwelcome suppliant; the object in question can always become engaged in intense devotion or a handy friend can intervene." Batrun ended, dryly, "Some girls are so devout they spend most of their time at worship."

"They have something similar on Vasudiva," said Ysanne. "But with men, not women. They worship Ap . . . Apl . . ."

"Apollo," said Batrun. "They use drugs and electric stimuli and mechanical implants in order to guarantee success. A short life," he mused. "But some would say a happy one. Well, Earl, do we rename the *Moira* the *Erce*?"

"No." He had no wish to advertise himself to others. "We'll call it—" he paused, thinking, remembering a certain small bundle of energy. "We'll call it the *Lucita*."

She had fallen and was crying, one hand clutching a skinned knee. A small wound, natural to all children with an active bent, but it caused Su Posta to blanch with the sudden fear of what might have been. A skinned knee but it could have been a ruptured spleen, a burst heart, a sharp branch which penetrated the lungs. Her fear gave birth to anger so that her voice lashed at the governess.

"Fool! Can't you take more care? Watch yourself, woman, or I'll have you flogged!"

Lashed, branded, sent to the mines. Things her mother had done to careless servants and she had done as much herself. To Lucy Hart, to Susan Schoo, to others who had betrayed the friendship she had offered; their disloyalty more hurtful than their actual crimes.

"My lady." As always Venicia was calm. "The hurt is small as is the pain. And Dana is not to blame. The child tripped while chasing a bird."

"You dare to rebuke me?"

"Never that, my lady." The bodyguard bowed, eyes masked to hide the fear within her. When Su Posta was in a rage no one was safe. "Shall I take her to the infirmary?"

"Yes—no!" She remembered the smells and terror of her own childhood. "I'll see to it myself. Bring me water and medicants."

Lucita stood and watched as the old hands dipped a handkerchief into the water and bathed the knee. A spray and the job was done, the wound sterilized and sealed against infection.

"Granny, why are you crying?"

"What, child?" Impatiently Su Posta shook her head. "What nonsense!"

"But I saw you." With the insistence of the very young Lucita pressed the point. "I'm not hurt, Granny. There's no need for you to cry."

"No, my darling! No!" The old woman yielded to temptation, hugging the small shape, feeling its warmth, the pulse of life running through the firm young body. "There!" She forced herself to push the child away. "Go and play now and be more careful!"

"Dear God, be more careful," she whispered to herself as the child raced away. "And live, girl. Live to rule!"

To take her place when she was dead and keep peace on Jourdan. To pick a consort and have a girl of her body to train as the following matriarch. As she had done and those before her since the beginning. A line which had faltered but had managed to continue and yet, now, the link was so weak.

That was a mistake she had helped make. Waiting too long to bear a child, losing the first, the second a boy despite the medications, the third a girl and then, after too long, Lucita's mother. But how to know that Sharon would have died as she had? To lie crushed and broken in the wreck of a raft after a picnic in the hills. And how to know that Sonia would have died in turn from an infection the doctors had not been able to cure?

Now, old, only she remained to protect Lucita and her right to rule.

How to keep her safe?

Distance wasn't enough and neither was her own presence. The hint of war on Lomund had sent her racing to safeguard the child and the memory of what had happened on the return voyage was still too painful to dwell on. If it hadn't been for a miracle they would be dust now and Marge Wyeth would be in her place.

Had she murdered Sharon? Infected Sonia? Arranged the sabotage of the ship?

She considered those possibilities as, rising, she restlessly paced the walled garden. The woman was a fool but there could be others behind her and, once in power, they could dispose of her in turn. Mikhail? Vasudeva? Fydor? Men yet they could have women in mind for the matriarchy—but could men have such courage?

"My lady!" The attendant had come on her unheard and now took a step backwards as she saw the fury in the matriarch's face. "An inquiry, my lady," she stammered. "From the treasury. A matter of your giving permission to settle a personal account."

"You intrude on my privacy for such a matter?"

"A formality, my lady. But you did ask to be informed should the matter arise."

Cowards, all of them, the woman quivering from the strain of simply doing her job. Was she such an ogre? Couldn't they see that all she demanded was cooperation? That and obedience, naturally, but people should obey their ruler.

"What is it?"

"This, my lady." The woman extended the scrap of paper. "Your promise to pay. Ysolto Mbushia, the Hausi, has come to collect."

Night on Jourdan was a time of softness. A thin skin of cloud veiled the cold glitter of the stars, turning their blaze into a nacreous glow which touched leaves with silver and turned the things of the day into products of gentle beauty.

Beauty Ysanne could appreciate. Standing at the head of the ramp she inhaled, breasts lifting beneath her fringed and beaded gown, eyes luminous as she turned to look at Dumarest.

"Night, Earl, a time of romance. It reminds me of home when we used to race beneath such a sky at the times of harvest. When the succuchi blooms filled the air with their scent and we'd pluck weed and chew and go traveling to magic places of the mind."

"And change lovers," he said dryly. "And fight."

"For joy, Earl, not because of hate. For the thrill of issuing and accepting a challenge. The pleasure of testing personal courage and skill. To us fighting is a game. A man will challenge another to fight for his woman or she will fight for him and, often, a man will fight a woman to prove he is fit to take what she will offer if he wins. It adds something to life, Earl. A spice. It gives love a deeper meaning."

"Love? You make it sound like rape."

"No, it's—" She broke off, then said, "Don't mock me, Earl. Don't ever do that."

"I wasn't and if you think I was then I apologize." He was sincere. "Each world has its customs and to each their own way. But on most worlds when a man fights a woman to possess her body they don't think it a game."

"But what else is it, Earl? To meet, to love, to enjoy each other?" Then, understanding, she said, "Oh, you're talking about marriage and children. That's different. When a woman decides to breed she picks the best mate she can to father her offspring. The crop can only be as good as the seed. That's really what all the fighting is about."

Badges of merit, token scalps, visible signs of battles won and status gained and, to the victor, the spoils.

As good a way to live as any if the environment permitted it. If greed didn't interfere. If the people could remain content with what they had instead of driving themselves insane with yearning for what they didn't need.

"Earl?"

"I was thinking," he said. "About what Andre told us of legendary worlds which survive unrecognized because of changed names. Like Heaven to Haveen. You must have lived in Paradise."

"No, Earl, Manito."

"What's in a name?"

Nothing that couldn't be forgotten in a woman's arms, the warmth of her kiss. Tonight she wore a different perfume and it filled his nostrils with an intoxicating scent, made him acutely aware of her femininity, the demanding heat of her body beneath the leather gown which felt like skin under his hands. In the soft light her eyes were pools of midnight, her lips parted, darker than blood, her teeth small glimmers in the open cavern of her mouth.

"Earl!" she whispered. "Earl!" She caught his hand and lifted it to her lips, their softness warm against his flesh, a gentle caress followed by one less than gentle as her teeth nibbled at the skin. A gesture betraying her mounting passion, induced by the mood created by the night. The mood shattered as footsteps echoed from the foot of the ramp. "Damn! Who's that?"

It was Ysolto Mbushia with bad news. He mounted the ramp at Dumarest's invitation, the silver light turning the cicatrices on his cheeks into a gleaming chiaroscuro. In the salon he said, "I'm sorry, Earl, but that note has been rejected."

"For what reason?"

"None was given. I didn't see the matriarch in person, naturally, I dealt with the treasury and saw only an official."

Ysanne snapped, "She could have lied!"

"No. Not to me. I know the woman." Ysolto took a sip of the wine Dumarest had poured for him. "I thought you'd like to know as soon as possible."

"The note?"

"Retained. I had to hand it in for verification. There was no trouble about that. No query as to its not being genuine. They just refused payment."

No money and no note—Dumarest's lips thinned with anger.

"What happens now?"

"About the note?" The Hausi shrugged. "I don't know. Usually the treasury is meticulous about settling accounts and it's obvious the matriarch intervened. At a guess I'd say you've lost out. Maybe you'd best forget it. Su Posta rules on Jourdan and you're hardly in a position to argue."

"Like hell I'm not!"

"As for the rest?" Ysolto Mbushia glanced at Ysanne then back at Dumarest. "The note was backing for the new generator you require. Without it the negotiations will have to be suspended. You realize my position? I cannot pledge myself to meet expenses without strong collateral. Now that the note has been denied you no longer have that. The goods you carry, the other things, they will meet the field charges, supplies and the cost of overhaul. There may be a little over for a certain quantity of fuel."

But there would be no generator and the ship was useless without that.

"The bitch!" Ysanne stormed in anger. "The old hag's doing this deliberately. Getting her own back for your having faced up to her. You saved her life and this is how she thanks you. So much for gratitude!"

"I don't want gratitude," said Dumarest. "I want what I've earned."

But how to get it? How to make a stubborn old woman keep her word? A woman who was the ruler of a world?

CHAPTER TWELVE

Could it have been Fydor? He had been on Jourdan when Sharon had died but so had Mikhail and Vasudeva and most of the others who would have any reason to have instigated her death. A dead end and she glared at the tablets lying on the desk before her, the small squares carrying names and dates and locations. Adjusted, placed in the right order, they should determine who had had the opportunity, the motive, the means.

Eliminate motive—they all had that. The means? She hesitated then decided all could have arranged for the thing to be done. Which left opportunity and that was no help at all because if they had the means their personal presence was unnecessary.

She'd come to a blank wall but stubbornly refused to recognize it. A computer could have handled the problem but then she would have had to confide in the technicians who would program it and they, in turn, could talk and so warn the one person she needed to catch unawares.

Again she manipulated the tablets. Fydor had been on the southern coast when Sharon had crashed and had been busy with a fishing project. Could he be eliminated? If so then Vasudeva was equally innocent and Mikhail had been too young for such devious machinations. Perhaps the accident had been exactly that and she was chasing shadows.

But Sonia?

The infection that had taken her life—could it have been deliberately administered? The suspicion had caused her to

125

send Lucita to Lomund and now it sent her hands flying over the scattered tablets, assembling them in various heaps, the highest of which should yield the answer to her search.

She had played this game as a child but now it held a serious intent. Lucita's life could depend on her skill and, with sick realization, Su Posta knew that her skill was not great enough.

"My lady?" Venicia was at her side. "The man Dumarest asks audience."

"Earl Dumarest?"

"From the field, my lady. He refused to be specific as to the nature of his business but hinted at a matter of the greatest delicacy,—which could touch your reputation."

"How?"

Su Posta hid her smile as the woman tried to be both knowledgeable and diplomatic. Any reason she gave would be a guess and it was simple to anticipate what one would be. A tall, strong man confined in a ship with a woman known for her tastes—did Venicia think her such a fool as to form an association with a blabbermouth? And yet even the possibility held a certain flattery, which she savored before putting the woman out of her misery.

"I will see him. The garden—in an hour."

She had always liked the garden with its winding paths and beds of flowers, its scented shrubs and the high walls which trapped the warmth of the sun so that the profusion of blooms which filled the air with their perfume seemed gifted with a special appeal. Here she had walked with her consort, now long dead, and here she had played with her children when they had been small. A haven of peace and one which held the tender memory of years long past. The residence of ghosts—one of which seemed to have taken form as Dumarest walked toward her.

A trick of the light—it had to be that. An illusion born of shadows and fading gleams but for a moment she thought Donal had come to her as he had so long ago, tall and strong and radiating a firm comfort. Then, as he stepped nearer, she saw the small, telltale signs which set Dumarest apart from all other men she had ever known. The hardness, the almost feral determination, the aura of power, the stubborn independence which had brought him to her as she had guessed it would.

"My lady!" He bowed as, coming close, he halted before her. "You are gracious to have granted me an audience."

"It would have been ungracious to have refused. Your business?"

"A small matter, my lady, yet one of importance to me. The question of a certain promise which—"

"You hinted of damage to my reputation," she interrupted. "Do you dare to threaten the Matriarch of Jourdan?"

"I would be a fool if I did."

"And you are not a fool. I understand your meaning. I still fail to understand your words as reported to me. Just what could you do to hurt my reputation?"

"Nothing." He was blunt in his honesty. "The words were used only to gain your attention. Now that I have it the real nature of my business can be mentioned. The matter of a promise, my lady. One you were kind enough to put in writing."

"The promissory note?"

"Yes, my lady."

"Which as yet I have refused to pay?"

"An oversight, I'm sure. If you will give orders to your treasury the matter could be settled without further delay."

"And if I refuse?" She waited as the question hung in the air. "If I deny payment?"

Dumarest said, coldly, "As you have reminded me, my lady, you are the Matriarch of Jourdan. If you refuse to honor the note there is nothing I can do. Of course the incident will be known and questions may be asked and, later, perhaps, your word will have lost some of its value. You may even feel a sense of—not guilt, for how can a ruler feel guilty?—but, shall we say, regret?"

"For a man you are bold!"

"My lady—would you have me cringe?"

So Donal would have spoken and, for a moment, the illusion returned so that she trembled on the edge of throwing herself into his arms. Then she remembered her age, who he was and why he was here. Not why he had come—though he might think it just for his money, but why she had forced him to appear.

She said, "I delayed payment on that note for a reason. I wanted to see you again."

"My lady, you had only to command."

"Perhaps. Or you could have been in space by now, but never mind that." Her gesture dismissed the concept. "My Akita are dead. Did you know their prime function was to guard my granddaughter? Well, never mind, they are gone and can be replaced in time but, until then, I have need of dedication and strength to safeguard the heiress. I have decided that you are the most suitable person to undertake the responsibility. Lucita likes and trusts you and you have proved your abilities. Shall we regard the matter as settled?" She frowned as he made no answer. "Well?"

Dumarest said slowly, "You honor me, my lady, but I cannot accept the assignment."

"You cannot?"

"I have a ship, others dependent on what I do, a mission to be accomplished." He saw the expression on the raddled face, the anger glinting in the eyes. A woman rejected—maidservant or matriarch the reaction was the same. Only the threat was different.

"You refuse?" Her rage mounted as he nodded. "How dare you! Who are you to put self above the needs of Jourdan? My granddaughter needs to be protected and I have decided you are the best person to do it."

"No, my lady—you are."

"What?"

Dumarest said, "You are her blood. Her grandmother. Her ruler. If she cannot trust you then who can she turn to? And you, my lady—you hand her life to a stranger!"

He was a fool. One who failed to recognize her power and his own helplessness. One who made no effort to mask his contempt. An idiot who had lost command of his tongue. Not even her late consort would have dared to speak to her like that.

And yet there was something heroic in his folly. Watching him, fighting her anger, she could sense it. So an early ancestor might have stood as he defied the elements; ready to die but unwilling to yield. Displaying a pride she understood only too well.

Then, abruptly, as if she had been looking through a kaleidoscope which had moved to form a new picture from the old, she saw things as they really were. Not an ignorant savage standing in stupid defiance but an intelligent man fighting to gain advantage. One who had deliberately manipulated her emotions so as to create the earlier impression. A gambler who had risked and won.

She wondered if he guessed how close he had come to losing all.

Watching, waiting his moment, Dumarest said, "My lady, why do we argue when your granddaughter is in such danger? The *Galya* was sabotaged as you must know and the target included both you and Lucita."

"Which is why I want her protected!"

"No one man can do that. You must have the loyalty of guards and attendants—don't try to abrogate your responsibility."

She said tightly, "Say that again and you'll regret it. Lucita is my life. Yes, I know you saved her and you'll be paid for it, that I promise. The note will be met the next time it is presented—but to hell with the money. I want the girl to be safe!"

And, desperate, she had turned to the one man she thought could insure that. Held him by stopping payment of a just debt, forcing him to come to her, exerting a pressure he had withstood and turned against her. Showing her, too, that she had been wrong. No single guard could give total protection. Not a thousand if the enemy was strong and determined and had ambition enough and wealth enough to achieve the desired end.

And Lucita, dear God, was so small!

"Think, my lady," said Dumarest. "Don't let emotions rule your head. You must have enemies—who are they? Someone knew of your journey to collect Lucita. Someone must have wanted you both dead. A person who had the motive, means and opportunity. One or—" He broke off, looking at her face, the expression it bore. "My lady?"

"Nothing." She had been thinking of the tablets cluttering the desk in her office. How strange that he had followed her own line of reasoning. "Go on."

"One or more who could have conspired to act against you. Maybe someone of your party was responsible and could try again unless stopped."

"Who?" She glared her impatience. "Give me the name!"

"I can't," admitted Dumarest. "I don't know it. But you could have the information to find it. Who rode with you to collect Lucita and did not return with you on the *Galya*? Someone who could have pleaded urgent business to take care of or who'd fallen sick just before departure?" He saw the change of expression on her face. "There was someone?"

Tammi Canoyan—the bitch!

"The handler was contaminated," said Dumarest. "A virus affected the brain and caused a mental breakdown. He killed the navigator and two others. Then he rushed into the engine room and tried to open the generator. It blew in his face. My lady?"

He stepped closer in his concern, but she waved him back and plumped on a bench, face mottled as she fought for breath. Fought too the rage which threatened to overwhelm her.

Sonia had died of an infection—had Canoyan been close? She remembered the tablets and, in her mind, picked and adjusted, setting each in its place to build a pile which told its story. The woman had had the means and opportunity, and the motive was obvious. With both herself and Lucita dead the direct line would be ended and the way open for her to claim the throne.

Canoyan, she was sure of it—but how to find the proof?

Dumarest had left at noon and now it was long after dusk with stars shining like beckoning lanterns in the dark immensity of space. Ysanne wondered what had brought such a poetic fantasy to mind. The lights were stars and stars were nothing but suns burning with fading energy until they finally collapsed to form white dwarfs or, if they had been large enough to begin with, black holes or red giants or even to explode in ravening fury as novas. These facts of the universe she knew the way she knew that the touch of the night wind held a chill not born of the weather alone, or that the silver sheen of the sky was not wholly due to distant stars.

Standing at the head of the ramp she shivered and tried not to think of another night when the sky had been like enveloping mother-of-pearl and the wind warm and Dumarest close. Remembered too the way she had felt and then found the pain of his absence was a knife in her heart.

"Ysanne?" Andre Batrun had come to stand beside her, his hair reflecting the silver sheen which gave it added luster. He looked tired, shoulders stooped beneath his uniform, the insignia of his rank as bright as his hair. "You're worrying," he said. "Don't. It's a waste of energy."

"So tell me how."

"To stop worrying?" He smiled and reached for his snuff, snapping open the lid of the ornate box and taking a pinch of the powder to stand holding it between thumb and forefinger. "One way is to keep so busy you have no time for anything else."

"Is that why you've been working so hard?" She waited until he had taken the snuff. "Is it?"

"Certain things needed to be done."

"I know. Instruments to check for the dozenth time. Supplies to examine, the structure to test, even the cabin doors to be renumbered. Make-work, Andre, and we both know it. The *Lucita*'s as ready as it will ever be."

The new name blazoned on the hull, stores stacked and the ship trimmed for journeying. Space was waiting—as soon as they got a generator.

"Ysolta was talking about the possibility of a cargo," said Batrun. "Staples to the mines then ore to the refinery on Myrtha. Little profit but it'll pay our way and we could haul ingots to Hago or Stave. Passengers too, and beasts—Craig's checked out the caskets. We'll take anything that comes."

And they'd go anywhere a profit was to be made. That was the philosophy of a free-trader, but the *Lucita* wasn't the *Galya* and, while Batrun was the captain, Dumarest was in command.

A fact she mentioned with unnecessary vehemence.

"I hadn't forgotten," said Batrun. "But a ship has to earn its keep. And while we're going where we're going it makes sense to get paid for the journey." He added dryly, "Especially as we don't know just where we are going."

"To Earth."

"Of course. To Earth. And have you plotted the course? Is it a five-stage flight pattern? A seven? Do we head above the plane of the galactic ecliptic or below? Which band? Which radial unit?" He saw her expression. "I'm sorry. I didn't mean to be sarcastic."

"Then why try?"

"A mistake. I'm not good at it."

He was trying to placate her and she smiled to show he

was forgiven. "Don't fool yourself, Andre—you're damned good at it."

At irony and psychology both; his induced anger had channeled her thoughts in new directions and dampened the nagging concern.

"Earth," she said. "We'll find it. It's just a matter of looking. Earl has clues. He mentioned them and will tell us more once we're on our way. Damn it, Andre, a world just can't get lost."

"No."

"No?" She had caught his tone and recognized the flat intonation as the question it was. "You think it could?"

"What if the name was changed?" He took snuff as she thought about it. "Suppose someone was looking for the *Moira*. Standing out there on the field at this very moment and searching for a vessel they knew existed. Would they find it?"

"The name," she said slowly. "Earl knows his world as one thing and others call it another. Andre! Is it possible?"

"It could be the answer. Why else isn't it listed in the almanacs? But that isn't really the important thing. Have you ever considered the possibility that, to Earl, the search is more important than the finding?"

He had read too much and dreamed too often sitting in the dim womb of his control room embraced by the placenta of his chair. The seclusion had affected his mind and given birth to strange fantasies. This explanation she knew to be false but she clung to it because the alternative was something she didn't want to think about.

Sound from below brought a welcome distraction; an officer with attendant guards who halted to stare up at the couple limned against the bulk of the vessel.

"Captain Batrun?"

"Here!" He looked at the military bearing of the contingent. "Trouble, officer?"

"No. Name me your entire complement." She nodded as Batrun obeyed. "It checks. Have everyone stand by for attendance at the palace at midnight. A special ball is being held to celebrate the escape of the matriarch and her party from death in the void. You are all invited to attend."

"All?"

"Your entire complement without exception."

Ysanne said anxiously, "And Dumarest?"

"Is already at the palace." The woman's tone was reassuring. "Don't worry about him. The matriarch just wants to express her private gratitude to her benefactor." She added, "The guards will remain to escort you at midnight."

CHAPTER THIRTEEN

Once, when a girl, her mother had taken her to see a forger lose her hands. The girl had been young and well-made but too ambitious for her own good. Trying to gain quick advantage she had forged bills of lading, using her body to seduce a willing trader, sharing the gains and hoping to build a quick fortune. A trick discovered after a hint from an associate. The sentence had been automatic.

Su Posta stirred in her high-backed chair, seeing again the slim wrists held hard against the block. The gleam of the blade as it had lifted to hang poised for long moments so as to increase the punishment. Then the sudden flash, the dull thud as the curved edge had bitten through skin and fat and flesh and bone to bury itself in the wood. The blood had gushed like fountains from the slashed arteries, splashing the attendants who had run to stanch the flow. Only when she had tried to move her hair back had the girl realized what had truly happened. Only then had she begun to scream.

The scream had echoed down the years, reflected in a thousand such punishments; scenes of scourgings and brandings and ceremonial maimings. The fruit of long-established tradition born in the early days when life was hard and incarceration a luxury they couldn't afford.

A scream she intended to hear again.

"My lady?" Dana had come to her as was her custom. "Lucita is ready for bed now."

"A moment." She needed the time to prepare herself for a

134

ritual she would no longer willingly forgo. Her own children had suffered from the neglect necessitated by the pressure of office but now, no matter what the cost, she would bid her granddaughter good night, give her a kiss, be warmed by her smile. Only when something is almost lost, she thought bleakly, do we really treasure it. "Is she alone?"

"No, my lady. Dumarest is with her."

He stood in a room furnished with a profusion of toys, legs apart, arms extended, hands hooked to grip the wrists of the girl who threw herself at him to be caught and swung and set down then raced again into his grasp, with gurgles of laughter and squeals of pretended fright.

"Granny!" She had seen the matriarch and the shape of the hovering governess. "Dana! Watch me swing!"

This time the squeals were louder.

A minx, thought Su Posta. Already learning to act, to attract attention and hold it. A useful trait for any ruler and one she must encourage even while disciplining the wild spirit the small body contained. Yet it was hard to halt her play and she waited until, breathless, Lucita screamed for mercy.

"That's enough!" Her tone brooked no argument. "Time for bed now, my poppet. Make your farewells to Dumarest and go with Dana to get your bath."

She came to him, wide-eyed and very serious, small hands on his as she said, "Thank you for playing with me, Earl. When I am older I'll take you for my consort. That's a promise."

"She could do worse," said the matriarch as the girl was led away. "A damned sight worse. I suppose you haven't changed your mind?"

"No, my lady."

"Stubborn," she said. "And a fool. You could have a good life here, instead you want to go off voyaging among the stars. What can you hope to find better than what I offer?" Change, she thought as he made no answer. Adventure and what the poets called romance. Danger and excitement and the novelty which was supposed to hold such enticement. For her as for any sensible woman such things were the stuff of foolish dreams. Adolescent yearnings quickly eroded by time. "You should have children," she said abruptly. "Take some advice—get them before it's too late. The wasted years can never be regained."

Advice given from the heart as he knew but he made no comment as she touched a fluffy toy, caressed a nodding doll which made thin, piping sounds. A parody of laughter which she found disturbing—how many laughed in such a manner as they mocked her behind her back? Too many, but they had to be tolerated as so many other irritations had to be borne—but tonight would see the end of one.

"My lady!" Venicia was at her side, her face smooth but her eyes revealing her concern. "You should rest. A warm bath and a few hours' sleep will help you to look your best for the ball."

"I can manage."

"Yes, my lady."

"You worry," said the matriarch. "But without cause. I'm not an invalid tottering on the edge of collapse and neither am I senile." That point she followed by a reluctant admission. "But perhaps a warm bath would stimulate me. Earl!"

She took the arm he proffered, leaning on it, as Venicia led the way to her private apartments. A strong arm; she could feel the hard firmness beneath the sleeve of his tunic and again she chafed at his refusal to obey her wish to guard Lucita.

"Stubborn," she said. "I sensed it from the first. Strong and, in my world, a strong man is not to be tolerated for long. Is that why I resented you?"

"A conflict of personalities, my lady," said Dumarest. "It often happens." He looked down into the face lifted toward his own, old, raddled, yet still revealing an iron determination. "No one likes to be dependent or beholden—and you are the ruler of a world."

"And you are a diplomat." She straightened as they reached her door. "Leave me now. I will see you at the ball."

It was a flamboyant affair with strident music and fancy dress and streamers, together with drifting balloons which emitted pungent odors when pricked, just as the food held surprises and the wine.

"Ugh!" Ysanne pursed her lips as tart astringency stung her mouth. "Stay away from this stuff, Andre. God knows what's been put in it."

Spices, she guessed, and herbs together with subtle flavorings and compounds which could loosen tongues and release inhibitions. Turning, she looked over the great hall. The tables were set on a raised platform which ran around the entire perimeter enclosing the dancers in a contained space over which they jerked in stilted movements.

Like robots, she thought, or mechanical dolls. Dressed and painted and following mathematically precise steps to the pattern set by the pulse of drums and shrilling pipes. Music not to her liking though the instruments were familiar. On her own world they would follow a different rhythm, catching at the heart and accelerating its beat with quickening tempo, the pipes a scream of released emotion echoed by the natural sound of those reaching orgasmic climaxes.

"Try this." Batrun handed her a goblet filled with a rich, dark ruby. "It seems to be normal wine." He sipped at his own then warned, "Be careful. You know you can't hold very much."

He stepped back as she nodded to allow a couple to pass close, the man wearing the costume of a bandit, the woman the plumage of a bird. Against this splendor his uniform seemed dull, despite the added touches of braid.

She said, "Can you see anything of Earl?"

"No, nor the others. Can you?"

Ysanne shook her head, braids flying. She had dressed them with ribbons and tufts of feathers and had painted her face with streaks of vermilion and orange, ochre and white. Decoration which, with her beaded leather, made her one of the costumed rest. Olga had worn only her faded uniform, Craig doing little more than mask his ravaged face, but Shandhar, more adventuresome, had adopted the garb of a trader in charms; hat, cloak and tunic covered in small metal symbols reputed to bring luck and ward off disease, guarantee success in love, war and the hunt and to enhance the chances of extended life.

"My lady?" A man no taller than herself looked at her with frank appraisal. "Will you dance?"

To refuse would have been impolite and she stepped down from the raised platform to the dancing area there to stand and move and respond to the stilted gestures of her partner in the artificial measure of the dance.

"You're a stranger," he said as it ended. "I can tell. That's

why I approached you—you have a charm our local women
lack. My name is Gergio Yate. And you are?" He frowned at
the answer. "Ysanne? Just that?"

"Isn't it enough?"

"For the purpose, yes, but it tells me so little. Nothing
about your family, for example. I could be talking later to
your brother and never know it. Or to your partner. You
have one?"

"If you mean a husband, no."

"I was thinking of a consort. Or perhaps a—" He broke
off, wary of treading on dangerous ground. "Anther dance?"

Again she suffered the mechanical tedium wondering what
pleasure anyone could gain from the stilted posturing. As the
music ended Gergio led her to a table where he began to se-
lect a variety of morsels for her to eat.

"Try this." It was a combination of nuts and sour milk
blended with a spice which tingled her tongue. "And this." A
paste of honey and flower petals bound with flour. "What do
you think of this?" Something which crunched as she bit it
and made her think of chiton and spindled legs. "And this
one really is unusual." He looked hurt as she rejected it.
"No?"

"No."

"Well, at least have one of these. They say they are the
matriarch's favorite biscuit."

It was small and round with a spongy center which yielded
a flavor of fruit and spice. A subtle burn which filled her
mouth with perfume and exotic tinglings.

Refusing another, she said, "Do you know her?"

"The matriarch? Not personally, but I know her by sight,
of course. You want me to point her out?" He looked around
the hall. "I can't see her but she's sure to put in an appearance
soon. But there's Maria Hutch!" He pointed to a woman who
glittered in a web of spun crystal flaring with gems. "She
owns most of the land fringing the Ferrado Lake and has
shares in the mines on Calvardopolis. A horrible place. And
there's Joan Gruber. She's almost as rich as Maria but far
younger. Even her consort wears clothing more extravagant
than that worn by the matriarch's late consort. A lucky man
but unless he's careful she'll replace him with another. Joan
has no patience with illness and he's been sick twice since

they came back from Hoorde." Gergio selected another morsel and, after he had chewed and swallowed, said, "If you're getting bored we could do something else."

"Such as?"

"Take a raft and go to the Chameon Hills. I've a place out there and we could spend a few hours searching for hilex and wild choum. Interested?"

"I might be."

"You'd love it. We could spend a few days if you wanted. At dawn the mists come to hide everything in purple veils and the hilex, when they wake, fill the air with soft susurrations." He stepped a little closer. "Please say you'll come."

For answer she nodded at a tall woman who had just joined the throng. One regal in a shimmering gown of golden threads which hugged the contours of her body. Long streamers fell from both shoulders and a tall hat crested a wealth of golden hair. Beneath it her face was hard, arrogant, wearing paint like a mask.

"Who's that?"

"Where?" Gergio looked to where she pointed. "She's Tammi Canoyan."

"Is that all?" She smiled at his expression. "No financial report or social status? Come on, Gergio, tell me something about her."

"She's rich," he said. "And ambitious. Some say she would like to rule. Treason, of course, but who can stop gossip?" He drew in his breath at a sudden flurry in the hall. "That's odd. The guards are closing the doors. I wonder why?"

Ysanne paid him no attention. She was looking at the matriarch, who had just entered the hall with Dumarest at her side.

The warm bath had helped but her brief sleep had been tormented by dreams so that now, despite her gown and the cosmetics masking her features, she felt old and vulnerable, her fear exposed for all to see.

"Steady, my lady! Steady!"

Dumarest was at her side, his arm firm beneath her hand, his voice a comfort in her ear. So Donal would have spoken at such a moment of crisis—but he would never have urged her to take such a gamble.

But was it a gamble when she had no choice?

"Silence!" Venicia called from her place at Su Posta's side. "Silence for the Matriarch of Jourdan! Our ruler by tradition and by right!"

A novelty, it had to be that. Ysanne heard the soft buzz of speculation as, leaving Gergio, she made her way to where Batrun stood with Craig, amid a glitter of medallions; Shandhar came to join them but Olga remained out of sight.

A blare of trumpets drowned the soft murmurings and in the following silence Venicia's voice rang with the clash of iron.

"I speak for my lady. Does any deny my right?" A formality and she continued, "The charge is one of treason against established authority. Of murder planned against my lady and her granddaughter during their return voyage to this world. To expose the culprit has this assembly been gathered. Does any question the right?"

Again the silence and then the soft whispering as questions rippled across the gathering.

"Madness," said Shandhar. "What the hell's going on?"

"It's tradition," corrected Batrun. "Trial by consensus."

"Either way it could be trouble." Craig lifted his mask and let it ride on his cropped hair. "And Earl's caught up in it."

"Hear me!" Venicia's voice lifted as the trumpets ceased their demand for silence. "Does any deny the right?" A pause, then, for the third and last time, "Does any deny the right?" A longer pause then her hand lifted to point. "Tammi Canoyan! Step forward so you may be judged!"

"What?" Anger flushed the cold features with a tide of red beneath the paint. "This is insanity. You accuse me of attempted murder. Of treason. On what grounds, for God's sake? I wasn't even with you."

"You were the instrument."

"Of what?" Canoyan glanced around for support. "The woman's gone mad, can't you see that? Who will she accuse next? You, Belle? You, Fleur? Let her get away with this and who will be safe?"

"You deny the charge?"

"What charge? I traveled to Lomund with the matriarch and her party. I fell sick and needed medication. The *Galya* left without me. Later when I'd recovered, I took passage to

Jourdan and arrived to learn the *Galya* hadn't arrived. I was as distraught as anyone at the thought of what could have happened. As relieved as the next when I heard of the rescue. Now I am being accused of attempted murder. Where is the evidence The proof?"

Dumarest said, "The proof lies in what happened and how it happened. Sabotage and the one who arranged it."

"Proof?"

"Some may think it so." Dumarest looked at the ring of attentive faces. "I speak for the matriarch but have no personal interest. I shall have no vote in the final decision. I am only—"

"Get on with it, man!" Canoyan was impatient, already tasting the final victory. This apologetic fool could have nothing but empty words to back the accusation. "Where is your proof?"

"It is circumstantial," admitted Dumarest. "But, I think, conclusive. The background is common enough; a ship chartered to conduct a party, a usual arrangement. But the handler fell sick after departure with a virus condition which affected his mind and caused him to run amok. He killed, was restrained, broke free and ran into the engine room and opened the casing of the generator. The point is—why did he run into the engine room at all?"

"He was mad. You said so."

"No," said Dumarest. "I said his mind was affected. It's only a guess but I think he must have been ill for some time prior to the *Galya*'s leaving Lomund. The condition could have sharpened his senses which is probably the reason he ran amok. An attempt to escape from overwhelming sensory stimulation." Pausing, he added, "The stimulation could have affected his hearing and that enabled him to learn something he was never intended to know."

"So?"

"A handler doesn't have much interest in the engine room. His job is to stack cargo, check supplies, take care of any passengers riding Low and livestock if any are carried. So what made him run into the engine room and remove the cover of the generator? To me there is only one logical answer—he tried to get rid of the device he knew had been planted there. The attempt triggered it with the results we know."

"So he heard something. What?"

Instead of answering the question Dumarest said, "Who would have been most suited to have set the device? It would need knowledge, skill and unquestioned access to the generator. Of the entire complement of the vessel the best person to do the job would be the engineer." Raising his voice, he called, "Guards! If you have arrested Olga Wenzer bring her here!"

She was still small, still brown, but now there was nothing meek in the way she stood and glared at Dumarest.

"Clever," she sneered. "You're too damned clever. Why should I have wanted to blow the generator? It was my neck too."

"Maybe not," he said. "I checked the sacs in the hold and one was equipped and supplied for a flight of long duration. And the handler jumped the gun. What if you'd left the *Galya* at a predetermined spot? The generator would have blown to leave it helpless but you could have altered course and drifted to a rendezvous, where you could have been picked up—maybe."

"Why should I have done all that?"

"That question bothered me but the answer lies in the records. Your sister was maimed for having stolen a collection of gems. Your mother was exiled. You have had good reason to hate the matriarch for years. Who found you, Olga? Learned you were a native of Jourdan? Got in touch with you and fed your hatred? Who suggested getting revenge?"

"No one!"

"So it was all your own idea? The device to blow the generator? The sac in which you hoped to escape? But there would have been no escape, Olga. You were to have been abandoned. Left to drift in the void, hoping for a rescue which would never come. Rescue had never been intended— dead you would no longer be an inconvenience."

"No!" She turned, her eyes, searching the crowd, setting on the tall figure of Tammi Canoyan. "No, she wouldn't—"

"Don't be a fool," snapped Dumarest. "What would she care about you? You're already frightened of her so why not make a clean breast of it? Tell the truth and the matriarch will be merciful—I promise it in her name. Why protect someone who would have left you to die?"

"Mercy?"

"I promise it."

"Then—" She turned, hand lifting, to stagger and slump, blood welling from her throat, the humming dart which spun in the center of a growing crater of cellular disruption.

The dart fired from the ring, which glowed like a baleful eye on the pointing finger of Tammi Canoyan's hand.

CHAPTER FOURTEEN

Standing at the open window Dumarest squared his shoulders and drew air deep into his lungs as he looked at the balcony outside, the expanse of the city beyond. The execution was over; Tammi Canoyan had paid the price of reckless ambition and was now nothing but a part of the heap of ash smoldering in the main square. He remembered the flames, the screams—Su Posta had not been gentle.

"It was necessary." She had come up from behind to stand at his side, guessing, with her woman's intuition, his thoughts. "An example had to be set to stop others from trying the same thing. A ruler dare not be gentle. And never forget that it could have been me out there."

He would but she would never rid herself of the fear she had known when, at the last, she had realized just how unpopular she had become. A gamble—so nearly lost! A word could have swayed the consensus to back her rival, a look, a tonal inflection—their faces had worn the feral hunger of beasts!

"It's over," said Dumarest, watching her. "Don't keep thinking about it."

Good advice but hard to follow. If Canoyan had fired at herself instead of silencing the engineer. If she had contained herself a while longer. If she had maintained her protestation of innocence—but the guards had prevented her from firing again and the dead woman had been proof enough of the accusation.

144

Details which now had no meaning. Dust to add to the rest, carried by the smoke, left to soil the gaudy pennons and streamers displayed throughout the city. It had begun to rain and in the dull harbinger of evening they hung like a collection of rags from their standards.

As she shivered, Dumarest reached forward and closed the leaves of the window. Wine stood on a low table and without asking her permission he poured, taking a sip before handing her the glass.

"Drink, my lady. It will warm you."

"And you made sure I knew you hadn't poisoned it."

"A custom on many worlds. Another glass?"

"This will do." She sipped, savoring the wine, watching as Dumarest moved about the room, sensing his restless impatience, his desire to be gone. "You still haven't changed your mind?"

"No, my lady."

"I shall not ask again." She finished the wine and set down the glass and looked at her hands, now so wrinkled and blotched where once they had been so smooth and vibrant with life. "All this means so little to you. An old woman, a child, an accident in space. Even the threat you did so much to solve. All unimportant. Just another episode in your travels. Soon you will have forgotten us all."

"I shall not forget."

"No," she admitted. "Only idiots and fools do that and you are neither. But you will not bother to remember. We shall be lost among all the other memories you have accumulated and, one day, when someone mentions Jourdan you will need to pause and think where you have heard the name before."

Memories, she thought, the sum total of existence, and he had so many while she had so few. Her childhood, Donal, others who had registered their presence on her emotions. Her children, Lucita—at least she could remember every tiny line of that small and wonderful face. Dumarest who had saved them both.

She said, "I must not detain you. But before you go there is a gift I must make. Here." She delved into a pocket and produced a heavy ring, which she slipped on his finger. From a wide band of gold the ruby stared at him like a watchful eye.

"Thank you, my lady."

"You will treasure it?" A stupid question and she was quick to rectify it. "Never mind. I am being maudlin. It is because I am tired. Venicia will escort you as you leave."

She waited outside and began to walk as he reached her, saying nothing until they had reached a passage in the lower region where she halted and faced him with an air of defiance.

"There's a question I must ask," she said. "The woman was your engineer—why did you accuse her?"

"She wasn't my engineer."

"Even so—"

"She begged for a berth," said Dumarest. "She was a skilled engineer yet she was willing to work as a handler. It only made sense if she wanted to hide. So I guessed that someone on Jourdan had reason to want her dead."

"Canoyan—the bitch!"

"So it turned out."

"You weren't certain?" She didn't press. "Well, she's dead now and that's all there is to it. But I had to ask."

A matter of loyalty, he guessed. Of the duty owed and returned by the one to whom it was given. To her it would be important, the code trapping her in a framework no less rigid than that which had led Canoyan to her death. The arrogance which had been as much a part of her as her skin. The inability to regard others as more than inferior. To consider herself inviolate because of birth and position.

Dumarest said, "I understand."

"Yes," she said. "I thought you would." Then, "Come, my lord. We haven't much farther to go."

Elge closed the door and leaned against it as he looked at the glowing depiction of the galaxy illuminating his office. A toy, it was no more than that, but on it one could build entire universes of fantastic complexity. The stars were not suns but solid balls of ice at the temperature of absolute zero. The planets not as cold but still frigid when compared to the smoldering energy of space. And beyond the galaxy, in the vast spaces between the island universes lay regions of heat so incredible as to baffle the comprehension.

A simple reversal—and to what realms of speculation it could lead!

Yet such a universe could exist and he had formulated the physics which would govern it. In this new regimen light was a variable governed by magnetic flux and temperature—variation. Gravity was a matter of pressure and life a facet of condensation.

"Master!" The voice came from his communicator. "Master may I attend you?"

Jarvet—why couldn't the aide leave him alone?

"What do you want?"

"The matter of the Illanian Combine, Master. Your final decision has not yet reached the programmers."

A moment, then, "Have all factories in the Harganian Sector of the Combine cease production of bacteroid 2427H. Within two harvests the blight it controls will have reduced the sector to starvation. Once that happens the Hegonians will have the lever they need to demand the dispensations they require."

"Yes, Master. And—"

"Enough!" Tedious detail when universes waited to be constructed. "Have all but urgent problems handled in the usual way. What news of Dumarest?"

"None."

So he had not touched at Millett or Emney as had been predicted. Which meant that an unknown factor had been introduced and with it a complexity of variables. Elge sat at his desk as he considered it. Where would he be heading for now? Or had he landed? If so, it had to be within a certain area of where he was last reported.

Those details clustered around his mind like bees around blossoms.

Later he would attend to them. Later. But for now there was more important work to be done. The last batch of recordings had to be studied and assessed before he could finalize his report to the Council. Obviously his previous conclusions had been at fault in certain aspects and efficiency demanded that he check and reexamine before crystalizing his findings.

The communicator hummed to be ignored. The voice of his aide echoed to be similarly treated. Then there was silence broken only by his own breathing, the soft rustle of his robe as he slipped lower in the chair. Silence and the shimmering glow of the depicted galaxy which filled the room with points of brilliance. Tiny fires reflected from the attachments of the recorder and turned them into things of brightness.

Jarvet saw them as he opened the door and lifted them from the shaven skull before looking at the man in the chair. Elge didn't move but remained with his face toward the profusion of light, his opened, unwinking eyes filled with reflected gleams.

"Master?" The aide received no reply and had expected none. Stooping, he waved his hand before the staring eyes then rested the tips of his fingers on the lids and lowered them over the glazed orbs. Activating the communicator he said, "Send Icelus to the office of the Cyber Prime."

He arrived within minutes, prepared for what he saw. With deft skill he made a preliminary examination then stood back. "Catatonia." His diagnosis was terse. "Complete withdrawal."

"There is no doubt?"

"None." Icelus lifted Elge's arm and released it. The limb stayed where he had left it. "You see? He has relinquished all mental control. The autonomic system of his body continues to function, naturally; if that had ceased he would be dead."

A word—Elge breathed, his heart beat, blood flowed through his organs but, as far as a living creature was concerned, he was dead. Without a mind he was little more than a vegetable.

"How?" Icelus looked at the attachments which Jarvet had removed and which now lay on the desk. "I see. You warned that something like this could happen. Did he leave notes?"

A tape to which they listened then; as it fell silent, Jarvet said, "It is obvious he became a victim of the same malady which had affected so many units of Central Intelligence. However he was certain that the condition was not caused by any disease or sickness. That it is, in effect, an acute heightening of the perceptions leading to an alteration in the viewpoint which leads to a change of mental frames of reference which had little or no association with the universe as we know it."

"A good definition of insanity," said Icelus. "What happened to his theory that the derangement was due to sensory deprivation?"

The tape gave the answer, Elge's voice coming in its even modulation from the speaker as Jarvet found the place.

"As a theory it has served its purpose and can now be discarded. From our experiments we have learned that there is a close corelation between catatonic withdrawal and mental ability. The higher the intelligence and the more disciplined the mind the greater is the ability to survive sensory deprivation. All cybers have a trained and finely edged mind. All suffer from some form of sensory deprivation for the major part of their lives. All anticipate the total cessation of bodily stimuli as the reward for dedicated obedience to the Cyclan. The laws that apply to emotionally crippled organisms do not apply to those free of such handicaps. The conclusion, therefore, is that the apparent derangement must be due to a growing awareness of mental capability on the parts of the units affected. To discover the real nature of this development is the basis of my experiments."

The tests and trials had ruined his mind, leading to the subtle addiction to madness that had brought him to his present condition. Jarvet looked down at the man whom he had served since his elevation to the highest office the Cyclan had to offer. Elge had failed, as his predecessor had failed, to find Dumarest and the cure of the affinity twin—who now would take his place?

Ysanne was restless, pacing the salon like a caged tiger, snapping at Batrun when he tried to offer condolences and reassurances.

"The old bitch has him fast and doesn't want to let him go. Soon it will be dark—another night and how many yet to come?"

"Probably none. Earl will be here as soon as he can."

"If he wants to come. If she hasn't bribed him with soft-bodied women—God knows she has enough at her disposal. Money too and—oh, the hell with it. I want a drink!"

She found it in a bar at the edge of the field and stood in a corner sipping a thick wine which tasted of oil and grease. Imagination, probably, but she forced it down hoping to numb her senses and quiet her nerves. She was acting the fool and knew it but the knowledge didn't help. Dumarest would come to her when he was ready and she had no right or reason to act like a jealous idiot. No wonder Batrun had thrown up his hands and gone to help Craig with the generator. Shandhar, too, had stayed well out of her way. He was a fool like the rest—couldn't he see she was concerned for them all?

The bar began to get crowded, workers coming in from the field, eager to shelter from the rain. A couple of guards entered, shaking rain from their capes, followed by a man who stared at her with frank admiration, another, more bold, who halted to take her arm. His companion drew him away at her frown; older, he knew what could happen to an impulsive male on a world ruled by women.

When the music blared from a machine, she'd had enough and went outside to feel the drizzle on her face. The wine hadn't had any affect and she guessed it had been watered or the pills Batrun had given her after the ball were still negating the alcohol. The palace drew her toward it and she was facing the door when Dumarest emerged. For a moment she stared at him and then was running to clasp him in her arms.

"Earl! I was getting worried!"

"No need. How are things at the ship?"

"As you might expect." She was chilled by his attitude. "The Hausi cooperated once the old cow met her obligation and met that note." She saw the ring on his hand. "A bonus?"

"You could call it that."

"Or a love-gift? I could call it that too."

"You can call it anything you want." Dumarest lifted it to look at the stone. "I call it fuel when we need it and supplies and stuff to help us on our way." He smelled her breath. "What have you been drinking?"

"They called it wine. I got it in that place at the edge of the field. Starrest, I think, some name like that."

"A dive." He took her by the arm. "Let's find somewhere decent so as to dodge this rain."

It was large, the room low-roofed, set with tables and benches. A tavern which held a warm comfort with windows that showed the darkening sky. A good place to be— compared to the other it was a palace against a slum. A youngster brought them a bottle dusted with sparkles and glasses engraved with interwound figures engaged in an ancient pastime. Pouring, he stirred the air with empty chatter.

"Did you see it? A public burning—I tried to get away but the mistress is strict and said I was too young and anyway, the place needed cleaning. I think she was afraid of my finding a better situation. The talk is that there could be more executions and if there are I'm going to attend no matter what. Not that there's much danger of losing my job. Once the word gets around we'll be run off our feet with the extra trade. A spectacle like that is bound to bring in the tourists. One thing you've got to hand to the matriarch she knows how to rule. Once let a rebel get a step out of line and who knows where things will end?"

"Bodies on every standard," said Dumarest. "Burnings every night. In a year you'll be famous."

"That's right." The youngster missed the irony. "Anything else, my lord?"

Dumarest said, "What have you to eat?"

"Some shredded meat roasted before an open fire and dusted with spice. Marinated fowl. Three kinds of bread and a soup so thick you could float a ship on it. If you want the full meal I could arrange a table in the restaurant or if you only want a snack you could have it here."

"A snack," said Dumarest. "Meat and some bread. Serve it here."

Ysanne laughed as the youth hurried away. "He must have heard of you, Earl. He acts as if you're his hero."

"No, he's afraid of displeasing you. Watch his eyes when he returns."

They flickered from her face to Dumarest and back again as if he waited a clue before speaking, as he put the food on the table and looked at the tip Dumarest had given him.

"Thank you, my lord. If there's anything more you want just let me know. We've fine rooms upstairs if you've the need for a soft bed and a bit of privacy." His eyes moved to Ysanne. "My lady?"

"Later, maybe. I'll let you know." Her smile widened as she followed the youth with her eyes. "I could enjoy living on a world like this. At least women aren't treated as chattels." She frowned. "Earl?" He had turned away from her to stare after a retreating figure. "Earl, is something wrong?"

"That man."

He frowned, trying to remember the fleeting glimpse he'd caught of the face. With deep lines and beetling brows, the cheeks blotched with purple scars, the face was not easily forgotten.

He'd last seen it on Zabul!

CHAPTER FIFTEEN

The field was heavy with dust, the *Lucita* a blurred shape to the edge and close to the fence. The ramp was down and Dumarest slowed as he neared its foot. At his side Ysanne glared her impatience.

"Hurry, Earl! The others are inside. If there's danger we've got to get in and seal the hull."

The obvious course, but Dumarest took his time. The ship seemed deserted, the area around devoid of life, if there was any threat at all it would be lying within the hull.

"You could have been mistaken," she said. "You only caught a glimpse of the man and he'd gone when I tried to spot him. At least I couldn't recognize anyone. Let's get inside and seal up."

"You go first," he said. "Give me three minutes then walk up the ramp. I'll use the emergency lock."

It engulfed him after she had entered to pass him through the hull and into the hold. It was deserted and he edged toward the engine room hearing small noises; the tap of metal against metal, the murmur of conversation. Sounds grew louder as he opened the door to show the newly assembled generator, the figures kneeling beside it. Craig and Batrun were apparently engrossed in their work, hands before them and hidden by their bodies. The tapping and murmur were as loud and as regular as before.

"Ysanne?"

"Here!" Dumarest tensed as he heard her voice. "I'm here—Earl! Be careful!"

The warning came too late. Dumarest heard the soft pad of a foot behind him, turned, felt the hard muzzle of a gun rammed against the lower region of his back.

"Move and you'll be a cripple," said Pendance. "Not really harmed but just unable to walk. Now do we talk like civilized beings or do I pull this trigger?"

He was as Dumarest remembered, suave, smiling, gems glittering on his hands, his clothing of expensive weave. A man who carried the odor of sweet flowers as if to disguise the stench of his chosen trade. He stepped from behind Dumarest as they entered the engine room to stand well to one side, Ysanne in the crook of his arm.

"That's better." His tone held a flaunting mockery. "You will never know how much I've missed you, my dear. The soft touch of your warm and demanding flesh. The pressure of your lips. Your words and passion." His free hand closed, fingers digging with sadistic pleasure into the mound of a breast. "Tell your new lover that, if he moves, I will turn you into a creature of nightmare." The gun moved to rest its snout against her jaw. "Do I make myself clear?"

A question Dumarest ignored as he looked around. At the generator the two figures remained as when he had first seen them. The noises he had heard came from a recorder, which fell silent as Pendance's companion touched a switch. Another he remembered from Zabul—how many more would there be?

"If you are hoping for the intervention of your steward then forget him." Pendance's voice held amusement. "Show him, Brice."

The man lifted a cover which rested close to the generator. Dumarest had thought it covered discarded components. Beneath it lay a huddled shape—Shandhar lying in the embrace of death, a small hole burned between his eyes.

"Was that necessary?"

Pendance shrugged. "Necessary? No. But he served as a convenient example to convince the others of the futility of resistance. And what need do I have for a steward? Steady, my dear!" His fingers dug deeper into the flesh beneath the beaded leather. "That's better. Just relax. Your turn will come soon enough."

"You followed us," said Dumarest. "How?"

"How could you think that I wouldn't?" For a moment

naked fury blazed in the opaque eyes. "To destroy my men and steal my ship—did you think it would be forgotten? For that alone I would have hunted you as long as life remained. Add the fortune you will bring me from the Cyclan and my own interests and you need ask no more." For a moment he savored his triumph then condescended to explain. "A detector in the control room was activated when you left Zabul. I managed to convince the ruler of that delightful world that it would be in his best interests to cooperate with me to the extent of lending me a ship so as to rescue those left in the ship you attacked. A neat trick and you are to be congratulated—the damage was greater than you could have guessed. However, here we are and all debts can be paid."

As Shandhar had paid. Dumarest glanced at him then at the other two. They knelt like statues, the prisoners of quick time. Seeing them, hearing the recording, Ysanne had lost her caution and run into the trap. Now there seemed no escape.

"The knife," said Pendance. "The one in your boot. A small detail, I know, but I'd prefer it to be settled. Remove it, Brice, and bring it to me." He smiled as, freeing Ysanne, he took the blade and examined it. "A good weapon, my friend. It holds many secrets. I think I shall keep it as a souvenir."

As he tucked it beneath his blouse Dumarest said, "You've a good hand, Captain, but not the best. I hold the aces."

"What do you mean?"

"The Cyclan want me alive and unharmed. Kill me and you get nothing." He paused, then asked casually, "I assume you are working for a cyber? You did mention a reward."

"A large one."

"But not large enough. Throw in with me and I can guarantee you triple what they offered."

"Words."

"The truth. Check with the cyber. Where is he? Was he killed?"

"Hurt, but not killed. I left him on Zabul." The gun in Pendance's hand moved a little as it pointed at Dumarest. "And you won't be killed. How would you like a new job, Ysanne? That of acting as a nurse to your hero. You'll have to feed him and wipe his mouth because he'll have no hands. And you'll have to move him about because he'll have no feet. No legs either. No arms." His voice deepened into a snarl. "At this moment I think it would be worth killing him for the sheer pleasure of it. Can you guess at what he's done to my reputation? I'd like to burn him inch by inch—but no matter. We must not let personal irritations stand in the way of vast profits. Triple, you say?"

"At least." Dumarest took one step forward. "Let me tell you about it. It's a—"

The lift of the gun checked him as he took another step. Pendance said, "Don't make the stupid mistake of thinking me an amateur, my friend. And don't think I'm squeamish. I'd as soon deliver you a cripple as not. To be frank it would be easier and I'm a man who has a liking for simple things. Now, you were saying?"

"I'm important to the Cyclan, have you ever wondered why? Think about it for a while. If you were to hold out they would raise their offer, but why take a part when you could gain a quarter? Easy money, Captain, and just waiting to be collected. I've the knowledge and we have a ship and crew. Two ships—yours is on the field?"

"Keep talking."

He was being sadistic and Dumarest knew it; letting hope flower so as to increase the hurt when he cut it down. This warped sense of pleasure had led him to become a slaver, to enjoy what he did. Now he listened, apparently interested, as Dumarest spun a tale of a lost mine on an isolated world, filled with gems of price and with rare minerals lying in eroded veins awaiting collection.

"All this wealth," he said when Dumarest fell silent. "And you didn't bother to pick it up?"

"For another?" Dumarest shrugged. "Why make anyone rich when you can have it all. A quarter, Captain, all for yourself."

"A nice thought and a generous offer," admitted Pendance. "But why should the Cyclan want a mine? The thought intrigues me. A half, you say?"

"A quarter—there are others to be considered. Isn't that so, Ysanne?"

She nodded, barely understanding what was going on.

"Three of us," said Dumarest. "Me, my woman and—" He moved to stand beside her, reaching out, one hand patting her stomach. "—the one to come. A quarter is all I can offer."

A child? Pendance stared at the woman then at Dumarest. Where he stood to one side, Brice licked his lips at the picture of wealth he had heard painted.

"We could try it, Captain," he urged. "Where's the harm in trying?"

"None at all," said Dumarest. "What have you to lose? And we'll count you in. Five shares and an equal split. One each for you two. One for Ysanne. One for me and the other—" Again he patted the woman's stomach, his hand rising toward the buckle, the knife it contained. "A deal?"

He moved without waiting for an answer, turning, the short, wicked blade gleaming as he drew it free; his left hand knocked up Pendance's right, the gun it held, the knife following the line of forearm and bicep to bury itself in the armpit.

To be twisted and withdrawn in a fountain of arterial blood. The stab once more. To rise bathed in carmine, to be thrown. To send Brice to join his dead captain on the floor.

"Here." Batrun dropped something small and round on the table in the salon. "The detector. Jud found it tucked in an air vent. Shall I destroy it?"

"No." Dumarest touched it with a finger, feeling the tacky adhesiveness of its surface. "We'll cycle it through the lock when we're in space." With Pendance and Brice now in sacs. If their ship should follow the signal it would find only the dead. A false trail which would yield valuable time.

The captain said, "About a cargo. I can get us a load—"

"No cargo," snapped Dumarest. "Not from Jourdan. We leave empty."

"Heading for nowhere with nothing in the hold." Batrun shrugged and looked at Ysanne as she entered the salon. "See a stubborn man. Maybe you should see what you can do with him."

"I know what to do with him." She sat as the captain left, one hand reaching out to rest warm fingers on Dumarest's own. "I'd like to give him everything a man could want," she said softly. "The home of his dreams and children to fill it. In the meantime I'll settle for what I can get. For as long as I can get it." Her fingers tightened. "More trouble, Earl?"

"No."

"Just says we can leave in an hour. No one's going to look for Pendance and his man. So why not take a cargo?"

"No cargo," he said. "And we'll change the name of the ship as soon as we can. Call it—" he broke off, then shrugged. "Call it what you like."

"The *Erce*." She didn't hesitate. "Andre likes the name and so do I. This time you don't overrule us, Earl. The *Erce*—it could bring us luck."

Luck to set against the risk of advertising himself to the Cyclan, but luck loaded with the possibility of gaining the attention of someone with essential information. A chance set against a risk but what was one more risk against so many?

How long must he run and hide and run again?

"No cargo," said Ysanne thoughtfully. "So no clue as to where we're going. And the changed name—more deception?" Her eyes searched his face as she added, evenly, "How close are they, Earl?"

Too close. Pendance would have communicated with the cyber left on Zabul and the Cyclan would know where he was and the fact he had a ship. An easier target to spot than a man but it gave him greater mobility. Again the setting of advantage against risk—all his life had been a similar gamble.

Ysanne said, "I'm not stupid, though I might appear to be so at times. And I can put scraps together to form a pattern. The Cyclan is looking for you and you're looking for Earth. Are they trying to stop you from finding it?"

That seemed a good enough explanation and he nodded.

"So they traced you to Zabul. Why did you go there? For information? What did you learn?"

"Nothing."

"Just that? Nothing at all?"

"I was kept rather busy," said Dumarest dryly. "Too busy to really question the Terridae. All I gained was a silly rhyme. Nonsense to do with a children's game, I think. At least that's what I was told."

"And you believe everything you hear?" She met his eyes, her own serious. "What was it, Earl? Can you remember?"

A thing heard once then drowned beneath a flood of action, but the data had been recorded by the machinery of his brain and could be retrieved. He sat thinking, throwing back his mind in an effort to relive the moment. Seeing again the wrinkled old face, hearing the thin, cracked voice.

"Thirty-two, forty, sixty-seven—that's the way to get to Heaven. Seventy-nine, sixty, forty-three—are you following me? Forty-six, seventy, ninety-five—up good people, live and thrive."

Ysanne frowned as he repeated it. "Are you sure?"

"I think so." Again Dumarest concentrated. "Yes, that's it. A number game of some kind."

"Or a mnemonic!" She reached for paper and a style. "A key learned in order to remember something of greater complexity. Now let me see." She scribbled, frowned, scribbled again. "Take the first line. Numbers can be spoken many ways so 324067 could be a sum total of an identifying number or even a code."

"A cypher?"

"Maybe, but I doubt it. That would add an undesired complexity." She scribbled again, gnawing at her bottom lip. "Three lots of six digits—what do they look like in a column? A row?" A moment then she shook her head. "It could mean anything but it has to be basically simple for it to be remembered. It must apply to something—but what?"

"The words?" Dumarest looked at the marks she had made. "What about the words?"

"Most probably they are a unifying doggeral. The figures must be the important factor. The figures?" Her voice dropped as she mumbled, "Three, two, four, zero, six, seven—Earl!"

"You've got it?"

"Drop the zeros and what do you have?" She shook her head at his expression. "Sorry, you're not a navigator, I am. Drop the zeros and you've three lots of five units. Navigational data, Earl! We don't use double figures because of possible confusion. So if I, as a navigator, say 'thirty-two, twenty', I'm really saying 'three, two, two.' Understand?"

She ignored his nod, burning with the excitement of discovery, eager to demonstrate facts he already knew.

"Think of the galaxy as a sphere," she urged. "A huge onion if you like. Cut it open and imagine it to be in layers. Nine of them numbered from the middle out. Each layer is divided into nine others and so on. Do you follow me?"

"Concentric circles," he said. "Eighty-one of them in nine separate zones."

"You've got it. Now take the first line; 3,2,4,6,7—we forget the zero. That's the third band out from the center, the second band from the inner edge of the third, the fourth from the inner edge of that and so on. That gives the first set of coordinates. The second lies on the plane which is divided like the rest. But how to tell which one?"

"The words," said Dumarest. He forced himself to be calm. "They must hold the clue."

Her lips moved as she read the doggeral. *"That's the way to get to Heaven."* We've found that. The next?" Her frown deepened. *"Are you following me?"* She looked at Dumarest then back at the paper. "Are you—" Her tone changed. "RU! Radial Unit! RU following me! Me? Meridian! The radial unit following the meridian. That means RU 1. And the rest? Up or down? North or south of the galactic equator? Which, damn it? Up or—" She broke off, one hand slapping the table to signal success. "Up, Earl. It has to be up. The words hold the answer. *Up good people live and thrive.* So that's it. We have the circumpolar location, the radial unit and angular position. All held in the mnemonic jingle." Her voice rose a little. "And remember where you got it from. Earl—these are the coordinates of Earth!"